SEAMAN

A NOVEL BY JAMES BRENNAN

First published in 1978 by
The Irish Writers' Co-Operative
27 Herbert Place, Dublin 2

The Irish Writers' Co-Operative has been formed
to provide outlets for new Irish fiction through
publications and organised public readings.

The Irish Writers' Co-Operative acknowledges the
assistance of An Comhairle Ealaion in the
publication of this book.

Cover design by Larry Bennett
Typesetting by Gifford & Craven
Printed by Folens Ltd., Tallaght, Co. Dublin.

To Pearse Hutchinson

CHAPTER 1

Mac rose from the wooden seat and began to walk round the lip of the pond. Busy ducks flung their bums to the sky looking for food. Nature's sounds were underscored by the ragged harmony of motor traffic surrounding Saint Stephen's Green. It was late morning.

When his tired feet brought him over the hump of the bridge, Mac turned to the right seeking unoccupied space. He sat under a tree facing an island and smoked. Drenched in a sudden sweat, his scalp itched and his feet smelt. Then, bored by the inevitability of duck's actions, and wishing to be out of the glare, he did the only thing he felt up to: he decided to go home.

He felt uncomfortable in the strong sunshine in full view of strangers, and when people looked at him he wished he were naked instead of enveloped in shoddiness, in clothes in which he was intimately aware of torn linings, worn soles and baggy hangings which obscured his external form. They'll never see me properly, he muttered.

— Excuse me, said a timid voice.

Mac stopped before a young woman and a younger man. A clean, wholesome couple, simply dressed and obviously virgins. Mac knew what was coming.

— Yes? he said.

— Do you believe in God?

Mac smiled at her frank expression of face and looked about at trees and flowerbeds.

— Yes, he said presently, but I don't feel that it really matters. He was looking at something over her shoulder. She shifted her head to catch his eye.

— Are you a Catholic? she asked.

— I don't know, Mac said slowly, I suppose so.

— Are your parents Catholic?

— Yes, Mac answered, sad at this mention of them.

— What made you fall away from the faith, she wondered, if you don't mind me asking?

Mac was looking at the young man's hips and thighs. Reluctantly he met her gaze.

— Fall away, he said, fall away. Is that what they call it? I don't see how it could have been any other way — not now.

— Look me in the face, said the woman. She was becoming sure of her ground and felt she could use a bolder tone with one of her own; which he was, she reminded herself, even if he had fallen away.

— Do you love God? she demanded, and nodded her head to make him say yes.

— Why not? said Mac. He lit a cigarette.

— And you know that he loves you? She smiled. It was a smile of complicity which is only given to a member of one's own sect and encompasses the identical knowledge you both possess. The young man nodded, affirming her statement.

Lazily Mac considered God's messengers. The frail, inexperienced bringers of the word. Surely they should be romping about on the grass in their supposed innocence, instead of questioning an old salt who was past all types of experience they could hope to understand.

— You will come back to the faith, the woman said. Promise me you'll come back to God.

The young man took a medal and chain from his breast pocket and moved near to Mac to drop it over his head.

— W-w-will you keep this miraculous medal, he stuttered, it w-w-will bring you back to the faith.

Mac liked instantly this stutterer with his charming gesture of magic, and with quick cunning put his hands on the lad's hips as if to steady them both. As the young man with raised arms brought the chain safely over Mac's unruly mane, Mac bent forward and simply kissed the fresh open lips.

For a moment all stood still. Mac felt a reaction run up the hips under his hands. As the young man backed away in confusion, the woman took his arm and marched him quickly off.

Mac turned towards the nearest gate, feeling that he'd gleaned something from the day. He allowed himself the fantasy that he was God receiving the charming stutterer's adoration. Frozen in almighty solitude he surveyed the lithe, prostrate figure and considered his work well done: he would resurrect that image at leisure later. Now he had need of all his senses in cheating the traffic.

Down Grafton Street's tiresome congestion where it was easier to walk on the road with monstrous buses nudging his behind. Overdressed people seemed frantic

3

about buying more clothes at twice the price. Absently he nodded back at faces he vaguely remembered. Faces of no importance to him, which always seemed to be there: part of the place.

His mind on the journey only. Over the wide bridge and left. Turn at the Flying Angel. Past Del Rio's and down Abbey Street to the Salvation Army. His life spent treading streets he didn't appreciate. A blast of river air and he was over.

The intellectual-looking gateman at Brooks Thomas's sat on his wooden chair as he had sat for decades on fine days, since before Mac was a thin, happy boy.

— Lovely day, said the gateman.

Mac nodded and went on past neighbours' houses to his front door. The neighbours were old, their children were gone; and all was quiet. He let himself through the red door and into the welcome shade.

He banged his hip against the handle of the brother's bike and stood still to enjoy the brief pain. He allowed the meaningless anger at himself to surge, and then to ebb further and further in faint widening circles until it was gone. Gone irretrievably as all other emotions on every day of his life made arrivals and departed and were no more, leaving him a little older and less willing to experience them again.

Mac was average height for a full-grown male, and had been described as uglyattractive. He didn't feel attractive today. The thin body in the shabby clothes was sagging into total prostration. Only the eyes betrayed the presence of enough will remaining to carry out the course of action he'd decided his life must now take.

He filled the kettle and lit the gas. He picked up a newspaper open at employment advertisements and put it down quickly: the narrow scope of his life could be read much too clearly in those lines which hindered dreams. That morning he'd hurried to an interview, with a carefully nurtured piece of optimism. But it was no use. He didn't know why he bothered – it was never him they wanted.

He made tea, put on a record, and reminded himself of his own instructions in dealing with depression: forget it, let mind go blank, get stoned if possible.

He was aware that most of his life had been wasted. All that time spent in boredom, or doing things he didn't want to do with people he didn't want to be with. The afternoons in cinemas, nights spent in pubs, schooldays of terror, and voyages in chains. He didn't know where to go from here. He had stopped battling reality and searching for ways out. He was tired. He knew he couldn't fight society any longer on its terms, and even if he could struggle on, the rewards were not what he wanted. In a meaningless life, the only thing happening was age, and age without grace was nothing to look forward to.

He recalled putting on the record, but not hearing it. He now chose some Indian music to play, and feeling hungry went into the kitchen. There were three cans in the cupboard – beans, peas and stew. He chose peas and sliced an onion. He cut up leftover boiled potatoes and threw the lot in a pan together. He said aloud:

– It's only a hash – keep me going till this time tomorrow.

He had a feeling of being overheard, though he knew the house to be empty. The family were on their annual holidays. He could not remember being alone in the house before with the rest of the family away. No, it had never been like this before. He felt that he shouldn't be here — as if he trespassed in the others' absence. The old house with its large rooms and high ceilings never seemed big enough to contain the family which lived in it; the only place where one could find peace and quiet was bed, and if it were daytime someone was sure to come bashing about looking for something.

The pan began to sizzle. He shook it to mix the ingredients and added pepper and salt. Indian music now penetrated the stillness with complicated rhythms on the tabla and numerous soaring notes on the sitar. It made him believe that life was being lived somewhere — frantically — as frantic as the beats on the tabla. But not here. Not in this drowsy city; this sluggish brown ebb of life like the slow river that ran through it. Life was going on here this timeless afternoon, but nobody seemed to be making an effort to see it lived. For a moment he imagined himself enveloped in a blood-orange sun at dawn, with an erection, awakened by this pulsing music and urged by the monstrous organ which filled the sky to commit, to partake, to live.

His hash was done. He dumped the mess on a plate and put the pan in the sink. He filled the kettle again. In the breadbin he found the hard heel of a loaf. With this in one hand and a fork in the other, he ate quickly. It tasted fine. All he wished for now was a bottle of stout and a smoke. Rising, he found the last bottle and lit a cigarette. The sour, tangy stout complimented the salty hash that went before it.

A cramp took hold of his stomach. He barely

made it to the lavatory, and had violent diarrhoea. Spasm after spasm passed through him for five minutes.

In the house again, the kettle was boiling. He poured the water into a large basin, added some cold, and placing the basin out of sight from anyone who might be at the factory windows facing the back of the house, he stripped and washed. Drying himself, he remembered an arrangement to meet Mona at six. He set the alarm for five-thirty, and carrying clock and clothes, he slowly climbed the stairs to bed.

CHAPTER TWO

He had finished the pint and was working on another when Mona swept through the door in that fast walk she had. Thin and dark, she stood with brightness shutting out behind her as the door swung to. She saw Mac and came across the dimly-lit lounge. Heavy velvet covered the windows. The carpet was vomit-coloured, and everything else was nondescript, down to the pussyfooting country boy serving the drinks. While she arranged herself on the plushy seat, Mac ordered a gin and tonic.

— You seem, she paused, different today. What is it?

— Ahh, he said, I dunno. The corners of his mouth were stretched down. She knew this could mean impatience, disgust or just a bad pint.

— You're fed up, she suggested. A cynical smile touched his lips, and he sucked his teeth sharply. She realised she would have to coax it out. Well — she had time. She relaxed, picked up the drink, and lips to rim, studied the barman. He had a handsome, dark face, but maybe a little too soft, she decided. An easygoing, goodnatured face, that accepted its place in the world and was thankful.

In contrast, her thoughts came back to Mac. Mac, the hard Mac. Hard and inflexible in his attitude to most things and people. With his weary expression of 'It's all been done', as if he carried three thousand years' weight of mistakes on his head. With his wild hair and sharp-angled visage. The keen grey eyes that met hers only for a moment – then flicked away; a patina covering them, suggesting a knowledge of every dirty trick in the book which he disdained ever to use. The outside eyecorners looked somehow squared. The long, full nose was bent. He was looking at the barman.

– Tell me something, Mac?

– What?

– I've always wondered what you – does that man attract you?

–No.

– Surely, she said, he would be considered hand-some? Look again.

– A face like an open country road going nowhere.

– Oh, come on. It's a very pleasant face.

– Pleasant? he said with bitterness. He's too old and too fat.

– You're mad. Well built. Mid-twenties, why . . .

– Old and fat – I'm old and skinny.

– Nonsense. You're built like a bull – if you'd stop drinking and eat.

– Can't eat.

– Mac, what are you going to do? The large head shot up. The eyes stabbed her face to see if she'd guessed: no, she hadn't.

— I know you, she said, you'd be happy to sit here brooding for the rest of your life — for God's sake do something and get out of this mood. Have another drink. She rooted about in the black leather bag.

— I can't get out of it. The words were slow, separated and emphatic.

— Here, she said, catch that boy and order another. Course you can, make an effort.

— I've made efforts, he said, I'm sick with making efforts. His tone put a halt to her gallop. She looked at his face. He was crying; large, squareknuckled hands on knees and a slow, even stream traversing the shaven cheek. She laid a hand on his.

— Mac, is it because of me? I thought you found it acceptable. You know: bottle of wine — bed. We didn't want anything more — well, it wasn't possible anyhow with Maurice and . . .

— Not you, not us — me. My mess. These relationships. . . . No matter how anyone feels about you, in the worst moments you're alone. Nobody can help.

— Mac, I'll help — if I can, I'll help. You're not that alone. You take an extremist attitude towards everything always. All women aren't me — you'll find a woman to love and she'll love you.

— Don't want a woman, Mac said, is that all you can talk about? He was angry enough at her presumption to stop crying.

— Well, a man, if that . . .

— No, no, that doesn't work.

— Alright, Mac. Mona felt the beginning of anger now. You've talked yourself out of the entire human race, which does leave you alone: now what?

— Give me, he said, twenty of the sleepers you use. That should just about do it.

— Mac, I can't.

The door opened. A soft breeze with a hint of mocking death and timelessness on it chilled the dim lounge. It felt like an undertaker's with an occupied coffin, where to make noise would be sacrilege. Mac's voice was lowpitched and lifeless, which further emphasized her creepy sensation. Too many gins in the afternoon, she decided, were responsible. A head rounded the edge of the door, studied them, and withdrew.

— It's not just a woman or wanting to be with someone, said Mac, it's everything. It's jobs I hate and can't stay at for more than a few months. Everybody's pettiness; the cosy little hells people make for themselves. The rotten way countries are run. The systems you can do nothing about: the way people accept it. But who am I to talk? The most I've ever done was told a foreman to shove it, and that only put me back on the unemployed list. It makes me throw up to do the jobs I can get. I'm sick of never having money. It's one shapeless, meaningless mess, and I don't know where I fit in. I'm interested in nothing but drink and sleep — and even then there are nightmares. I feel so old.

Suddenly weary, Mona went through the motions of ordering more drinks.

— There must be something you can do, she said, some work with satisfaction.

— Then please tell me about it. Tell me where — what — suggest.

— It's not my fault, she replied to his sarcasm. Go away somewhere.

— I've done that, he said, get a job, get a room, and then get lonely. All anyone's interested in is how much work they can get out of you. That's the game, and if I don't like it I can piss off.

— But Mac, everyone has to make a living.

— The dead don't.

— Intelligence doesn't absolve you from the dreary day-to-day necessities of the world. It never did; if anything it makes it worse. You carry on through all the futility, wars and wasted lives — that's part of it.

— For what?

— For whatever one wants. Mona was losing patience.

— I just want to die peacefully. There's nothing going on in this world I want enough to pay this price for. I mean, what is it that people think they want? This dream of the perfect mate, the love affair that lasts a lifetime: it doesn't work that way. Money, it's all filthy, and where I've seen it, it buys only a safer brand of boredom. Children: the thought of having a child who even might one day feel as I do about life makes me impotent, and the change-the-world-by-revolution vocation would be laughable if it hadn't already caused so much suffering to millions.

Mona was surprised by the ease with which he expressed himself — she hadn't realised he could so clearly. She'd thought of him as a — usually incoherent — mumbler. She felt guilty for not having concerned herself more about his life. During the time she'd known him, what she had considered directionless, wasteful brooding had, she now realised, been a consistent analysis, culminating in this moment. So that when they'd made love, how close to this decision had he been? There must have been a part of him coldly surveying what he called his mess of a life even as she experienced the warm joy of copulation. These thoughts she found saddening; they seemed to make of all their time together a waste.

She allowed in their silence a process of distancing to grow. She didn't need to concentrate at it, once the feeling began to clarify itself. He developed in her mind as a separate entity, which he'd not done before. Before this, her memories were of a give-and-take of time, place and personality, with no defined separateness. Looking back, she spotted clues to his state of mind, which she'd not paid attention to at the time. His evasions: he would talk himself out of anything; a job, a philosophy or a sense of optimism, by negating the thing ingeniously down to a bitter yet comic absurdity. It had become one of his habits to make use of these evasions when needed. He covered the tracks of his motives for doing nothing with elaborate contradictions. He took a tormented pleasure in continually masturbating his discontent at his inaction, and could turn this into orgasms of horror by thinking of what his acquaintances would think if he took an action or said anything which aroused their conservative scorn.

She knew he had the wrong friends. He was trying to conform to their drunkards' cynicism, but he would always be considered different and he knew it. What could she say now? She didn't know where he would fit in any more than he did himself, and if he preferred their company to loneliness, what about it — most people preferred any sort of intercourse to loneliness. That they sometimes laughed at him she knew, but not to his face. And how could she now enlighten him

13

about this, and let him die with the added humiliation of knowing himself to be considered ridiculous by his so-called friends?

She was convinced he would die somehow because of his honesty. He was fundamentally honest, despite the evasions and subterfuges he'd used. For if evasions had worked, and kept on working, he wouldn't be in this position now. Any kind of lie could be used (and is used daily by millions) to stave off the decision Mac had made.

Though she'd never had this brand of depression, she couldn't escape the logic of his solution. Life had given her problems of a sort which she'd known she could overcome with effort because she could see and believe in the rewards for such efforts. The way Mac presented his case, his problems were insoluble, and he was past believing in rewards.

If she were asked afterwards why she went on trying with him, she couldn't have answered, but try she did, although by now she felt the outcome of all this was a foregone conclusion.

— Postpone it, Mac, just wait — do nothing. I know some people who'll give you a job.

He was shaking his head.

— What about Ricky — where is he?

— Poncing about the south of France.

— You spoke of him before as if you loved him. Isn't it possible again with someone?

— What have I got to offer? Mac's hand gestured palm-up between them. Love, he said, love. I believe a fifteen-year-old when he says he loves — at least, that's how old I was when I experienced something like that. After that it means nothing. I don't see how anyone could love me. I'm far too old and horrible.

— That's not true at all.

— Then marry me.

— Mac, that's not what you want.

— No, but you've never wanted it either.

— This is getting ridiculous — you've no right . . .

— Nobody, Mac said, has any rights in relationships; that's what makes it all pointless. If both sides don't agree to endless compromising, it doesn't work.

— It's not like that. Don't go believing that. Love is . . .

— Don't sit there ranting about love, Mac cut in, I know you used to fake orgasms.

— God damn you!

— He already has, replied Mac, and while we're at it, where's your husband?

— I'll not discuss that with you.

— Hah. What difference does it make now?

— Maurice, said Mona with resignation, was — is — a cretin, but it was satisfying that way.

— Somehow it can be better with someone you don't give a damn about and will probably never see again. That's how it's been with me. Meet someone and as long as you're in a hurry to get to bed it's all right, but afterwards, or when you meet them again and there's nothing to talk about, and you go to bed again as a matter of form, it becomes pathetic. Stripping and going through the motions in a room even if the passion's a bit soft. You turn him over, and looked at he's not the beauty your imagination had you see in the bar or under the streetlights. Not the great love you defied the state, the church and the hearth to find. Just an ordinary joe with nothing to say. Damn it, most of them don't even try to make it exciting. For excitement you have to go back to one young enough, who still has a sense of sin; one with a trembling passion, who yet believes he shouldn't be doing this, and he might change his mind halfway through, or be so ashamed after I feel terror at the thought of his initation; you're caught by the short hairs no matter what way you turn.

Mac paused — drank. Mona sat looking at her glass. Mac continued:

— The exasperating thing is that I know it should be male and female, but I'm not capable of staying with a woman — it becomes boredom. And the sight of some women with their babies, their cooking and their little men I find saddening. It's their unreasoning complacency, the unthinking knowledge that what they are doing is so right, so natural and there's no way they can be wrong, even if they're the worst of mothers and their children turn out to be monsters. That's what kills me about these females; I can't forgive them that lack of turmoil, the bliss on their faces, the fact that they have made their place in the proper scheme of things and are never likely to lose it.

— They suffer too, Mona said.

— I suppose so, but it's not the same agony.

— It certainly isn't, I . . . Ladies, she said, and went.

She sat in the windowless box. Face flushed, brain swimming. Angry, for she'd never heard anyone speak of women that way. The cheek. But, she told herself, she must calm down. She did so, looking at the mirror where someone had squeezed out their pimples. She mopped her face with a tissue. Suddenly it occurred to her that he might be able to write. She

16

half-rose from the seat — then sat back: he hadn't the patience. What on earth would he write about from that abyss? That negative hell he was in wouldn't entertain a maniac. That he wasn't mad she was sure: there were no signs of that. What to do? What to do? Keep on sitting here and maybe he'll go away.

No, it solved nothing and anyway he wouldn't. In his condition he'd sit anywhere forever, brooding until she returned. Dammit! But she sympathised. He was capable of suffering more than anyone she had ever known. She made up her mind. Give them to him. With the means in his pocket he was sure to review the situation and anything could happen to change his mind in the meantime. She went back in.

— Go to a doctor, Mac, she said as she sat down.

— I'm not sick.

— I mean for the pills.

— He'd guess my state of mind and refuse. You're the only one I can talk to — I can ask. When I try to tell the others they buy me another drink and tell me to forget it. Give me them. No-one will ever know where they came from. Mona, I know what I'm doing.

— Christ, Mac, couldn't you rob banks or something like these other cowboys?

— I don't want to interfere with anyone's life, I . . .

— You're interfering with mine. He was silent. The loungeboy cleared the table. When he'd gone, Mac said:

— I must have the choice. I must. If you don't I'll do it another way.

— Okay. I'll give you some. Tomorrow, here — at eight.

He was nodding his head: — Thanks, thanks, he said, thanks. Have another drink.

CHAPTER 3

The south quays stretched from Butt Bridge to Ringsend. A long, deserted mile, with old warehouses, coalyards, a few pubs and a church facing the river Liffey. Halfway down, towering over the cranes and ships' masts, stood the huge, green gasometer. The tethered, silent ships hugged the quay walls. Nothing moved on the black river.

Mac walked by the stacked-up tanks of Guinness; the blue and cream ship alongside, waiting to export them to England. Down the cobblestone quays was his favourite walk. Most of his early life was associated with the river. His grandfather, who used to net salmon long ago, told nim stories about boats and the river when Mac visited him. And in his backyard, giving substance to the legends, were three long oars standing in a corner, and bits of fishnet and old ropes with big, striped cats sitting on them sniffing fishheads. Mac had been fascinated by the river from the first day he had seen it. His grandfather had always promised to take him out in the boat when Mac was bigger. By the time he was big enough the boat and gear were sold. The only thing left were the oars in the yard, dried up and warped, and his grandfather sitting, looking into the fire, fishing in his pockets for tobacco.

Mac finished a bottle of wine and threw the bottle into the river. He was opposite City Quay Church. The tiny grey church where he had joined the Boy Scouts at ten. With the clean, uniformed, well-behaved scouts, he had marched up to Burgh Quay to get the bus for a hike in the mountains. 'Be prepared', he remembered, was their motto. And the gangs of dirty kids jeering at them as they paraded on Sunday mornings after Mass. 'Don't pay any attention to those scum,' one of the scoutmasters used to say. At first Mass, one Christmas morning, a scout fainted. Don't break ranks, the scoutmaster said, and sent two patrol leaders to carry him out. Jesus, said Mac, did I really do all that?

He opened the other bottle of wine. There's the pub where I bought that first flagon of cider at the side door. How old was I then? Thirteen. Someone else was with me. Can't remember who it was. We got merry behind a crane before going to the pictures. The first real drink. How the world, and everything in it, sparkled that night! Buying two Players in the little shop. Smoke half of one on the way to school, tap it, put it in your pocket for later. That horrible last year in school. They considered me dense. Brother Hennigan, a long streak of misery with blue tinted glasses and one shoulder six inches above the other. From Cork, he was; no other teacher in the school could hit you with such precision and strength. Trying to learn; history in Irish, geography in Irish, even religion in Irish. I couldn't speak a line of Irish to save my life. And his blue-eyed boys in the

19

front row. He used to slip them sweets.

I developed migraine that year. Stand up in class, expression of pain on my face, point to my head and get excused. He used to hate me at first, then he forgot I existed. It was better to sit outside with migraine than look at the loathsome bastard all day. When I left school the migraine disappeared forever.

Mac sat on a steel bollard. The ship that was tied up facing where he sat flew the British flag from her stern. She was a huge ship; her black-painted side rose twenty feet above the quay. It was quiet, with only an occasional car going by to break the silence. Further down, under the next crane, a shadowy figure was picking up the lumps of coal that lay scattered about the quay.

A taxi pulled up behind Mac. Four men got out. They were drunk and shouting.

— Pay the robbing bastard and get rid of 'im. How much does he want?

— Shut up and let's find out.

— I'll break his thieving neck if he charges too much.

The one doing most of the shouting was young. He was about six foot three and had a bushy red beard. He danced around the taxi in jerky movements as if he were shadowboxing. The oldest among them paid the taximan. He was quiet, thin, small and wearing a blue suit. The others were dressed in denim jackets and pants. All had different accents.

— Where's the women? redbeard roared, looking around the quay. I had that little blondie one, she said she was coming back with me.

— C'mon aboard, Corky, that was hours ago. You

went an' got too drunk again.

The man in the blue suit said this as he went towards the gangway.

The wine bottle was snatched from Mac's hands and thrown into the river.

— That oul' wine will rot your guts. Come aboard and have a decent drink.

Mac let himself be pulled off the bollard and steered towards the gangway.

— What do ye think of those bitches uptown? They let you buy drinks for them all day an' then disappear when you're drunk, Corky shouted in his strong Cork accent, peering into Mac's face, his eyes mad with drink.

— Happens everywhere, Mac said.

Mac was perfectly at ease going aboard the ship with the drunken sailor. He had spent eight years at sea himself, and ships to him were homes. He was not afraid of the huge, bearded Corkman. He had known men like this before; when sober they behaved like big, gentle children. I might as well be here as anywhere else, he was thinking as he climbed the gangway behind the unsteady Corky.

The deck was littered with tangled ropes and pieces of timber.

— Watch your footin', Corky warned as he tripped.

Mac helped him get up. Inside the accomodation they went along a narrow alleyway.

— In here. They turned into the messroom. The man in the blue suit was taking plates of food from a hotpress.

— That's the last bloody meal I'll be cookin' you lot of maniacs, he said, putting the plates on a table. I'm payin' off tomorrow and I'm not comin' back to sea again.

Mac sat down and took the bottle of beer Corky had given him. He had heard that last sentence a million times before. Jimmy Lestrange used to say it every trip, when Mac was a galleyboy on the 'Old City of Dublin'. Jimmy, who learned to cook while he was with the Irish Brigade in the Spanish Civil War, drowned in Rouen on what was definitely his last trip. He fell between the ship and the wall one night; couldn't find the gangway. The propellers churned him up from the bottom three days later.

— How long have you been out, Doc? Mac asked.

— Two years on this one and I've saved every penny. I'll be in Liverpool tomorrow night and I'm not leaving it again.

— You'll be back to sea, Doc, Corky said, you'll get fed up ashore after a few months. Corky was waving a chickenleg in the cook's face.

— Not this time, lad, not this time, Doc said.

— I'm telling you, Corky shouted, you'll be back.

— Eat your dinner, lad, and don't be worrying about me. The cook helped himself to a beer from the case on the table. One of the others who had been in the taxi suddenly fell asleep. He fell forward, face into the plate of food.

Yes, thought Mac, calmly looking on at the scene, this is exactly how I remember it to be. Those countless nights in countless ports when I staggered aboard, cursing a taximan, cursing women and cursing the world. The world of ships in dockland. A mountain of hard steel, with a flag on it representing where you came from, the place you came from representing order, reason and decent whiteman's morality. But here in dockland none of that applies, neither do the laws of the foreign country. A situation like this one, in Mac's experience, usually ended up with lots of drunks fighting each other. Mac had memories of three and four day drinking bouts when it seemed that the entire ships' crews of fifty men were roaring drunk and doing the weirdest things. In those situations the best thing to do was stay ashore until the ship was due to sail.

Mac found it peaceful there, listening to the old cook. When Corky finished eating he staggered out of the messroom with a beer. They heard him arguing with someone in the corridor.

— He's a good lad, is Corky, the cook said to Mac. He's headstrong, never stops to think. He'll always be in trouble. He reminds me of my old dad. He was from Cork. Once he got an idea into his head, off he went. No-one could talk to 'im. He'd listen to nobody. He'd keep on shouting what he was trying to say, over and over, all night. He was convinced that no-one really understood what he was shouting about. So he'd shout louder. Just like Corky. The cook was smiling.

— Don't you get fed up with someone like that, Mac asked.

— I get fed up, but people like that got to be looked after. Someone has got to be with them and looking after them, otherwise they get into trouble. It's our duty to look after our mates. You can't leave people like Corky alone. They can't deal with the world.

— What happens when you're not around?

— Then I'm not responsible, the cook said. I remember the last time in Bremen. Corky and me went

23

up to Smokey Joe's for a drink. We were having a nice few beers when Corky discovered his jacket was missing. Which one of you jewburning bastards took me coat, he roared at the bar. He'd left his money in the coat, but that's not the way to go about getting it back, is it? I thought they were going to murder us, them Germans. The barman let loose the big dogs he kept in the back room. Corky kicked one and it lay down. The other stood over it crying. The barman came for us with a policeman's baton. I had to drag Corky out of there. Well, I'm off to me bunk. Help yourself to a beer.

— Thanks, goodnight. Mac hadn't been listening to the cook's story of what had happened in Bremen. He'd been thinking about what the cook had said earlier; people have got to be looked after. Obviously, the cook reasoned that if everyone looked after the people in their immediate vicinity, then everyone who needed help would get help.

But what kind of help was that? The go to bed, everything will be fine in the morning philosophy could only satisfy a fool. Mac admired the old man for bothering; many didn't. But keeping someone like Corky out of trouble while you happened to be on the ship with him was surely a wasted effort. Corky was going to find or cause trouble wherever he was, and help of the cook's kind would only prevent him from dealing with the real trouble — himself. Here I go again, figuring out other people's lives. Trying to be a social worker. That time I went to a psychiatrist on the National Health; what is it that has you depressed? he asked. The second world war, I said. You weren't even alive then, he said after checking my age. What difference does that make? I asked, anybody who isn't depressed about the second world war is really sick.

An hour later he handed me packets of pills. Go out and get a job, he said. You'll be better off working. It will take your mind off the war. Go to work and take the pills. I was doing that before I came to see you! You're supposed to help me. The pills will help you, he said. Goodbye.

The whole business is a waste of time. Useless. Hate yourself afterwards for telling them anything. And the terrible comedown when I stopped taking the pills. I was sure that gangs of old ladies were following me everywhere and were going to kill me with their umbrellas. And every busdriver was trying to run me down. When I felt threatened, these huge, black waves seemed to be piling up, ready to drown me. Standing there, unable to move, helpless in the middle of the street. If I didn't drown I was going to be run over by a bus. It got so bad I was afraid to leave the house.

What is it that frightens me? It's nothing I can name. Nothing frightens me . . Nothing frightens . . Nothing.

CHAPTER 4

Mona Fulham sat down with her back to the windows of the restaurant. From here she could watch the door and she had easy access to the ladies' room. She would have to pay a visit soon, considering the amount of drink she'd had today. It had been an exhausting day and it wasn't over yet. First thing that morning her mother had called her from the States.

Mona stood at the phone on the cold landing, still groggy from sleeping pills and freezing in a pair of panties, frantically lying, answering her mother's concerned questions.

— Hi, dear, it's mom. How are you?

— Oh, fine, just fine.

— You sound as if you have a cold.

. — It's a bad line, mom, really I'm fine.

— How's that husband of yours? She always chuckled when she asked about 'that husband'.

— He's fine too, you missed him by a few minutes, he goes to the office at nine. God, if she only knew.

— Your father's been ill again . . . well, can't you say something?

— Eh, yes. How is he?

— He'll be all right. It was his heart this time. He kept asking for you.

And on and on for twenty minutes. Repeating the questions over and over again. 'Are you okay?'

— Yes, mother, I'm fine.

Mona was shouting.

— Don't be angry, dear, I worry about you so much.

— Mother, don't start crying, please, it's very nice of you to worry but there's no need. I'm fine and I miss you a lot.

— Okay, dear, as long as you are well. Bye bye.

Every two weeks her mother called and put them both through it. The calls were always the same. Her mother and father were well into middle age and believed that Mona, an only child, should stay near them. Her mother had never liked the idea of Mona going to Europe and it was only after Mona had gotten married that she had stopped pleading with her to come home every time her father was ill.

The waitress had been standing beside the table for some time. Mona came back to the restaurant with a jolt. The clock said nine fifteen; Justin was fifteen minutes late.

— Would you like to order?

— Yes, please, a carafe of white and a beef curry. You can bring the wine now.

With her hand curled around the wine glass her mind drifted back over the day. After her mother's call she lay down in bed to get warm. Her husband Maurice, whom she hadn't seen for a week, was flying to Hamburg today on business. She was to meet him at six for

27

a drink before he left for the airport. Dear Maurice, she didn't feel angry about the situation any more. It was even funny sometimes when she thought of the change he had undergone. He had been a long-haired stage-manager in London. A twenty-four-year-old dope-smoking, beer-drinking, slightly scruffy stage-manager in jeans — having a drink with the far-out cast and back-stage people in Nottinghill Gate after the show.

Mona had flown over to London to spend a week-end with an American girlfriend who had a part in the show.

The last performance had been that Saturday night. The cast had pelted the audience with ten pounds of raw liver. Then the cast, the audience and the crew had milled out into the street; an hysterical mob of hun-dreds running around the theatre to finish up. The show had run for six weeks and had gotten good reviews. On Monday, after a two-day celebration party, Maurice and Mona came back to Dublin, and were married within a week.

Back in Dublin he had given up theatre. He said there was no future in it. He took a job with an import/export company. Now, scarcely a year later, one could hardly recognize him. He had joined the army of sleek, well-dressed 'whizz-kid' businessmen who jetted around Europe making deals. She hardly ever saw him, just a quick drink between flights. He had sounded urgent over the phone this morning; maybe he had made up his mind about a divorce. Oh, well, she would find out soon enough.

After her mother's call she had sat staring out the window, a crisp new sheet in the typewriter; fingers poised over keys, and wanted to put on a record or go out for a drink and forget the heartbreaking business of writing altogether. She had made a tremendous effort to concentrate, staring at the page. It had blurred and she was going over the conversation with her mother again. Damn her damn calls. How can I write when I get her whining calls first thing in the morning? Another day and I can't write. How many days make six months? Wrote my first book in three months. Every day nonstop for eight hours. That was at home – the midwest in summer. Mother bustling about making coffee all day. Telling the neighbours that in the next room her daughter was writing a book. When it was published they were all so proud. A month after, she was packing for Europe. Do you expect me to stay in this hole all my life she'd shouted at her shocked mother.

A year later Mona sat watching a robin pecking on her windowsill. She'd been married and was sure she was going to be divorced. All this and I'm not yet twenty-four. But that's not the worst. The worst is, I can't write. She'd screamed at the robin. She'd taken two tranquillizers and found her book of phone numbers. Justin McGarry. 94104. She'd rung the number. She'd forgotten when and where they'd met, but remembered him giving her the number. He hadn't published anything in years. He must be over sixty now, she'd thought. His best works were written thirty years ago. He probably won't remember me.

After what seemed ages he'd answered. He'd remembered. Yes, he'd said. Tonight. She'd told him when and where and hung up. He'd sounded lonely and a little amused by her panicky voice.

The day had moved faster after that. She had

taken a bath, washed her long, black hair and brushed it fine and glossy. She'd even poured a glass of wine, and stood before a print of Emily Bronte drinking a toast to herself. Then she'd gone to meet Mac, expecting to relax for an hour before meeting Maurice.

Christ, why couldn't Mac keep his depressions to himself instead of going around laying it on everyone? Did he think life was so easy for me? Obviously he did. He thinks I'm a success story — a published writer. Author of a silly, badly-written two hundred pages about a girl who gets pregnant in college. Even if he read it he'd still feel the same. Thinks nobody suffers the way he does. I'll give him the sleepers — frighten the shit out of him. Then we'll see whether he means it or not. He's probably out getting drunk again with the rest of the hopeless cases.

After Mac, she'd met Maurice. Maurice avoided her eyes, insisted she drink brandy, and looked important in his gray mohair suit. He'd finally learned how to attract a waiter's attention.

— Two brandies. Doubles. He'd snapped doubles as the waiter turned away. He'd looked at his watch.

— I'll get straight to the point. You and I . . . I don't think . . . How can I put it — perhaps we were hasty.

— If you want a divorce that's fine by me.

Her voice had been too loud; the waiter must have heard. Maurice had looked relieved and embarrassed. He'd drunk down his brandy.

— Good, then that's settled. How are you?

— Oh, for God's sake, Maurice, you don't care — why ask? If you must know, I feel lousy. She'd finished her drink. He'd signalled for two more.

They'd drunk in silence, both of them staring at the ashtray on the shiny table. They'd spent five minutes like that, then Mona had stood up and walked out.

Justin McGarry stood at the restaurant table, looking at Mona. He saw a young woman staring wide-eyed at her plate, with a piece of beef speared on her fork. She's not beautiful, he thought, but it's a good square honest face. He liked the combination of black hair and dark blue eyes.

At sixty-five Justin was still tall and straight: in his youth he'd been a well-proportioned giant. His strong face was beautifully sculptured, and showed little sign of his age. Something about the stiff crop of white hair and the set of the mouth gave the impression — despite his slow movements — of a dormant vitality.

Mona shook her head and lifted the fork to her mouth. She raised her eyes and saw him. She put the fork down again and blushed.

— Excuse me, she laughed and blushed, I'm not with it at all this evening.

He found her voice pleasant.

— It's me who should be excused, he said, I've kept you waiting.

— Please sit down. Will you drink some wine?

— I'll always drink wine with a lovely young woman, Justin said, and watched her mouth widen into an unsteady smile.

— I'm glad you came. I was afraid you'd think me presumptuous, having met you only once.

— Not at all, glad to. What's on your mind? he asked. Her mouth and eyes betrayed her worry.

— I can't write. She said it simply; stating a fact.

31

Her mouth began to tremble. Justin smiled. He felt tenderness for her like an ache in his chest. How exposed her soul must have felt saying those three words. Three words with such a terrible ring of finality to them. He took her hand in his own.

— Mona, listen to me, there is nothing to worry about. Every writer has felt that at some time. Especially after the first book. You will write again, and write well.

He gave her the reassurance and encouragement she needed, yet still she looked worried.

— There is something else?

— Yes, but I'm not sure I should bother you with it. She looked up at his face and then the words came out in a rush:

— It's this friend of mine, he said he's going to kill himself, and I don't know what to do. I've no-one to . . .

She stopped, waiting for the soothing words as before, waiting for someone she felt to be stronger than herself to take command and say 'This is what we'll do' with authority in his voice. Justin sat silent.

His mouth was set tight and his eyes became cold. He shifted around in the chair away from Mona. The pleasurable evening had come to an abrupt end. The mood of inertia and despair that had taken hold of him more and more this past year settled down over his mind. It settled like a sodden, heavy fog coming in from the sea, rolling over the city, along streets and alleys, down into cellars, up steps and clinging around chimneypots and spires.

He had fought this mood with strength, and with the tricks he'd learned over a long and varied life, and up to ten years ago this life (apart from the wars) had been abundant with everything nature and the world had to offer. Fame, money, travel, good health, and the woman he'd lived with for thirty years and loved. Now the woman was dead and he'd no wish to live with another. His last book was dead and he'd no desire to write another. He wandered around the city with nothing to do, passing the time.

And lying sleepless at night, when even the brandy failed to bring him dreams, he went back over his life from the stone and saltwater fundamentals of his beginning. When his bare legs had more strength than the run of the island could use up. When his thoughtless appetite sated a scalding hunger after a day fishing the wild Atlantic. When in innocence he knew nothing mean or despicable about his relatives or neighbours, and all loved him for it.

Then the priests' college which couldn't contain his imagination. His wandering — the awful jobs. World War I. The civil war which made him despise half his race and leave the country for being full of bigoted incompetents. And after the worst came the best — discovery of his talent. The great power he harnessed. The energy he put into books. The ability in stories to place each faultless word in perfect clarity. But all that was a long time ago, and past glories didn't amount to much in the present. And after all the idealism for a better world was gone; after the stupid wars that changed nothing, you had done what your nature had you do, and then . . .

— All things must die, he said, half to himself.

Mona had been watching his face, intently waiting for his answer. Hearing this, she drew in a sharp breath.

—'What? Is that all you have to say? For the third

time that day she was angry with a man. — He's twenty-five years old — doesn't that mean anything?

— If he hasn't the will to live, then he might as well lie down and die. The world doesn't need people like us.

He had not meant to include himself. He shrugged: it would have come out sooner or later.

— What do you mean by us? Mona's eyes were wide open, darkening rapidly with suspicion. — You? Jesus! She spread her hands over her forehead. I come to get help for one and I run slap bang into another. What's going on?

— Look, I shouldn't have said that, you're upset enough already. Please calm down, try to forget I said it. It was stupid of me.

— Forget it! She took her hands town from her face and looked at him. You sit there with a drink, calmly telling me I'm to forget it. Is this all a joke? Is everyone pulling my leg?

Justin sat there silently miserable. He scratched his scalp absently with one finger, and looking at him she knew that it wasn't a joke. Just as with Mac earlier on, she could sense and nearly smell the aura of defeat that clung to both of them.

A picture came into her mind of very still bodies, and she felt the cloying chilliness she associated with the dead, and shivered. She could not speak now, and as if in a dream she watched him stand up and say something she could not hear. His mouth moved soundlessly, his empty blue eyes looked through her. There was a roaring in her ears like being in a fast train going through a tunnel. His mouth stopped moving. He turned away and walked out. She sat staring at his glass.

It still had some wine in it. He has used that glass, she thought, his lips touched it, his hand touched it. He has been here; the glass is evidence. Tomorrow he might not be, but tonight he sat in this restaurant and drank from that glass.

Because she could not hear his voice just then, her mind conceived of him as already dead. A spirit. Her shocked senses doubted that he had been there and said the things he had said. Her memory tried to erase itself of Mac and Maurice and Justin, but the glass was there before her. It had happened. The roaring stopped and she heard again the restaurant noises. Knives and forks scraping plates, the murmur of conversation. She sat there for a long time.

CHAPTER 5

Mac forced himself to slow down when he had turned the corner. He looked behind to see if any of the prowlers had followed him from the toilet. No-one had. It could be embarrassing when one of those people recognized you in the street and you didn't want to talk to him. Anyway, what was there to talk about? They were not friends. They were shadows on a piss-house wall, whose destination was total loneliness. How many of them were there in the city? In the world? Combing the city's toilets every evening after work until they closed. 'Queers' was what the kids they were chasing called them, with malice. Then what do those kids think of me? Mac stopped dead, the thought had never occurred to him before. If that's what they call them, then that's what they call me. To them I'm just another Queer. The way they said it in Dublin, twisting their mouths, the very word conveyed disgust. Mac was horrified. He seemed to see the faces of his family floating past his eyes, saying 'queer, queer', and then his relations, 'queer, queer', and his childhood friends and their families, until there was a host of people, everyone who knew him in the city, chanting 'queer, queer', with disgust. Oh, God, was it possible? Remember, Dublin is a small city. Mac leaned against a wall. He was drenched in sweat. His knees felt weak. He was staring at the pavement under a streetlamp, when the pictures appeared. One moment he could see a large grey paving stone, then the stone would blur and like on a movie screen the faces appeared. His dead grandmother was sternly shaking a finger at him. After her, a fierce uncle was threatening to break Mac's back if he ever interfered with his children. The faces faded and he was staring at a stone again.

Mac began walking again quickly. Mac walked everywhere quickly, even when he had nowhere special to go, so that he arrived everywhere in a sweat. He galloped along furiously, keeping pace with his furious thoughts. He could not kill time; time killed him. Everything he did had to be done as quickly as possible, no matter how badly, do it and get it out of the way. He was so impatient to be everything all at once, he never got around to doing anything. In his imagination he mapped out all sorts of glorious careers for himself, and abandoned them all as soon as he realised they would take time and effort. His indecisive mind gave him agony. The weighing-up of every little action contemplated. 'Will I or won't I', 'Should I or shouldn't I', 'Is it worth it,' and so on until finally he would take action in a fit of bad temper and get no satisfaction from doing it, or, as most times, talk himself out of it altogether.

Mac now found himself in the neighbourhood where he had been born and spent the first eight years of his life. He entered a huge square with tall red houses lining three sides, and a national school of the same colour on the fourth side. In the centre there was a playground and football pitches. In the playground Mac sat facing number twenty-seven. Between the house and the river there were coalyards, and beside the coalyards the gasworks. Mac could smell the gas and almost taste the cinders which crunched underfoot all around. The lights high up on the gasometer threw a dull shine on the summits and slopes of black coal mountains. It was very still, and quiet, and chilly. Number twenty-seven looked back at him, high and silent. The broad steps leading up to the hall door, which Mac remembered as being covered with children, telling stories and singing under the streetlamp, were empty. Where are the children? It had seemed to him that there were hundreds, more than he could ever count, filling the square all day and far into the night. Maybe there are no children living here now! While he was sitting there, not a soul had come in or out of the houses. It was dead. Just another dockland.

Mac felt cheated. He had expected other generations of children to continue the cycle, to live the first eight years here and feel as he did about it. To keep alive what he thought were unique street memories. Every street was different: when Mac was eight the kids two streets away were thought of as foreigners.

But even then, Mac remembered, the exodus to the suburbs had already begun, and somehow, those kids belong to the city. Here we go again, working over the old working-class pride. It's still in me, thought Mac, still there. Mac's working-class pride allowed him to consider anyone who was not brought up on a city street to be worthless. Those past few years when he caught himself feeling this resentful pride he tried to put it out of his mind and look at people, whatever their background, with an unprejudiced eye, but it was hardly easy. Ironically, he couldn't bear to be in the company of someone who had the same prejudices as himself. This had happened with his family. It was difficult for him to be with people when every time they opened their mouths he heard a clear echo of a part of himself. When a part of himself he didn't like was echoed, he disliked intensely that person whose mind was so like his own. These thoughts in common, which could be so delightful when shared with someone not of the family, made him rage inwardly in the home. He did not want to be so like those he was in such close contact with.

A ship's whistle blew going down the river. How often he must have heard that sound, so close, when living here. He closed his eyes and tried to reconstruct one or two scenes of what it had been like here over twenty years ago. The back room in number twenty-seven he could see clearly. He was lying in his wooden cot. Through the end bars was the fireplace, on one side the big bed, and on the other the wall. There was paper on the wall which you could scratch and tear off in strips. He could taste the bitter varnish when he chewed on the bars of the cot. He could hear the radio and the bells from beyond the window. He could see his father laugh over at the fireplace. That was all he could see. He stood up, and walking from street lamp to street lamp, left the silent empty square.

Mac was sober again and angry for wasting time with nostalgic memories. He wondered if other people spent as much time as he did with their memories. When left to himself he could brood for hours, remembering his life back to the cradle as if searching for some key, some moment of illumination he might have had at one time, which he could now use to unlock a door into a future. But there was no key, there were only good memories and bad memories, nothing really worthwhile hanging on to. Better, he thought, to have the whole lot programmed completely out of your mind, and devote all thought to present and future. But Mac didn't like thinking of the future; the present was unbearable and the past was safe because it had already happened. He hurried back to the pub through streets haunted by memories, streets on which he had spent countless nights walking himself to exhaustion. He didn't walk about at night now, he drank himself to sleep. Jesus, it was a mistake to come down here, he reflected; when I think of all those times that I was looking forward to something, running around Dublin hoping it would all change, hoping that somehow, someday I would never again feel the lifelong hopelessness that these streets make me feel. Looking at the streets and the shops only makes those pointless years hang more heavily. The waste of time, the sheer fucking waste when I wasn't even enjoying myself. What makes me return again and again to a city and its remembered streets where I can only travel backwards to the hopelessness I felt which made me leave it in the first place? Goddam these streets. Godddam the changing, never changing, clinging memories of this cheating city.

CHAPTER 6

— Let's get food and wine and whiskey and drive out to the mountains and have a picnic, Anna said.

— It's ten o'clock at night, Mac said.

— So what? We can all go to the beach and take our clothes off and drink and fuck and get blasted.

— We can get blasted here and go on a picnic tomorrow. That way we can get blasted twice, Mac said.

— You guys sit here in the same old bar every night. Let's get a case of whiskey and just fuck off into the mountains, or watch the ocean for a week.

— Too tired. We'll have a few more pints and think of something later on.

— Paddy's got some heroin we can shoot up.

— Later.

— Look at all these weird people. What do you think they're doing?

— Getting stoned.

The pub was packed. The three barmen couldn't give out drinks fast enough. It was bright and warm in the large room after the chilly streets. Mac felt like sitting here forever.

— Imagine spending your whole life in a pub, said Mac to Anna.

— You do spend your whole life in a pub.

— I mean twenty-four hours a day, every day.

— I can't imagine. It's too boring. You're pre-occupied with the pubs and the Dublin drinking trip.

— What are you going to do with your money?

— If you like we can sit and drink it here twenty-four hours a day for the rest of our lives.

— For the rest of our lives. What's the rest of our lives?

— I don't know. She stressed the 'I'.

— It sounds like the title of a television serial. Mac had the feeling he could see and hear what went on in the pub but he was not actually there. It was like watching a play — 'Life' happening on stage. No matter what occurs up there it can't physically involve the audience at their safe distance. This detachment Mac was feeling about the time and place he was in made the things that went on around him in the bar seem unnecessary. The gestures, the shouts, the passion with which the inebriated customers expressed themselves became absurdly comic.

— Did you ever try to kill yourself? he asked Anna.

— Did you want to hear the story of my life? she countered.

— Yes, it would make a change. Can you make it sound real?

— Once upon a time in Chicago, four immigrants from mid-Europe ran a kosher butchers. They realized they weren't getting anywhere fast being kosher butchers so they went into the bootlegging business and became millionaires. One of them was my father. I received a strict Jewish upbringing and four years ago at twenty-one I got my share of the loot. I left Chicago and came to Europe. I married a Swede in Paris and when he left me being pregnant, I tried to kill myself. I took an overdose and passed out. When I came to three days later on the concrete floor, my right leg was paralyzed. Lying on the concrete had done something to the nerves at my hip. Now I'm sitting with one bum leg, drinking with you in Dublin.

    — How did we come to be sitting here talking?

    — We started talking when we saw each other here one night.

    — Yes, but how did we know each other? I don't want to talk to everyone that comes in here.

    — Some people recognize something in each other and start talking. We are two of these people.

    — It happens so quickly. Yet I seem to have known you were always there. Like it was inevitable that someday we would meet. This sounds like the great confession of love in "Gone With the Wind".

    — We know we are not in love.

    — Yes we know that. But we are fond of each other.

    — What does fond mean? asked Anna.

    — I don't know, said Mac, but we are fond of each other. Is life really like it is in Beckett's novels, and are we deluding ourselves most of the time, or is there really any point in thinking about it? Having said that, Mac took a long swig at his pint.

    — Mac, you're getting too heavy.

— But you must have thought about it.

— Why think about it. Get stoned.

— But someone has to think about it.

— Why?

— I don't know.

— Then why think about it?

— Let's get another drink.

— That's right, one thing at a time.

— Let's drop some acid?

— O.K. Here's yours and one for me. Down the hatch.

— Let's break all the rules? We'll sit here and smoke a joint.

— O.K. Light one up.

They washed the acid down with some fresh drinks and smoked the joint.

— It looks as if we might enjoy ouselves tonight, Mac said.

— I'm beginning to feel better already. It's good hash. Wait till the LSD hits, Anna said, and rummaged in her bag.

— Want to snort some coke?

— Sure. But don't make it too obvious, you never know who's looking. Mac was getting nervous.

— Maybe we better keep it for later?

. — O.K. Keep it for later.

— How are you feeling?

— Fine. Let's take it easy for a while and go back to the house later and play some music.

— O.K.

— Hi. A young man wearing tight pink trousers sat down facing Mac and Anna.

The young man looked at them, shifted his

pink-bound crotch a little to the right, and laughed.

— What are you doing? he asked.

— Oh, just sitting here, Mac said.

— What's happening? Anna asked the young man.

— Nothing much, wish I was stoned.

— Here, light this joint up. Mac handed over a joint. He was too lazy to light it himself.

— What's your name? Mac asked when the joint was lighted.

— Jim, said the young man with a smile.

— You've got a lovely bum, Mac said.

— Well, I think I better be going. The young man stood up.

— O.K. Jim, it's been nice meeting you. He stood up and put his hand out.

— Bye.

— Bye.

They shook hands and after waving to Anna the young man left.

— Who was he? Mac asked Anna.

— I dunno.

— Jesus, the people you meet. That man is still talking to God over there. He's been at it for hours.

An old woman started singing. Her high, quavering screech demanding and getting silence. All hands stopped talking and gazed into their pints as the virtues of some young, dead patriot were extolled in ballad form.

— I thought singing wasn't allowed, said Anna.

— It isn't. She gets special dispensation on account of her part in the troubles or something, Mac explained.

The ballad ended. The drinkers clapped their

hands and the general uproar resumed as before.

Mac spotted pink pants talking to a male friend in blue pants and said —

— Would you like to come down to the toilet with me for five minutes.

— Fuck off, said blue pants.

Mac went back and sat down beside Anna. He spent the next ten minutes gazing at the lovely way pink and blue pants moved until they both walked out of the door.

— Isn't life wonderful Anna?

— Yes Mac, wonderful. But why give those kids such a hard time?

— I, eh...

— Will I tell you why? Anna paused, looking into his narrow suspicious eyes. You hate them because you don't look like them anymore. You hate them because you think they're stupid. You hate them because they won't let you fuck them and even if they did you'd hate them because afterwards they'd call you a queer. But you don't ever hate yourself, do you Mac? You poor, sorrowful bastard.

She was right. He knew she was right by the way her words hit him, as body punches hitting under his heart. So that's what other people saw it as, he thought, his mind running quickly back through a series of embarrassing images. Why didn't someone tell me before? His face reddened.

— Mac, I'm sorry. He shook his head and lay back in the seat with one hand over his eyes. He felt his soul was fully exposed to all. His own, very personal, only-to-be-looked-at-in-the-strictest-privacy soul. That part of himself he considered with a shy, foolish smile, or with dreadful solemnity.

— Mac, I meant what I said in the best possible way. I hope you understand that.

— I do. It's a shock to hear someone say it.

Mac was aware that a frightening intimacy was developing between this outspoken woman and himself. You could trust an American to give it to you in the face, he thought, whatever it was. Her blunt truthfulness was new to him, and it shocked. He didn't know where, if given the time, this nearly too truthful intimacy could lead.

As the drugs began their work his mind ceased calculating. He turned to her with a slight surge of hope.

— Let's go to your house, he said.

— I'll call a taxi, Anna replied.

CHAPTER 7

Anna's suburban house was the most badly kept on its road. Beside it, every other house seemed pretentious. The front garden ran wild; the hall door was weathered to a faded red with not the slightest hint of polished brass; the curtains looked as if they had been something else before becoming curtains.

Inside there were plain white walls and not much furniture. A large plastic bin stood in the kitchen at the back door. It contained many different types of empty bottles. In one corner a bottle of gin was the cargo in the back of a child's toy truck. Mac sat on the ravaged couch. Anna poured two large glasses of red wine and turned on the record player. The record began revolving; the needle protested loudly about some scratches, then Greek music leapt into the room.

For half an hour they sat, sipping wine, soaking in music, saying nothing. Mac was mentally sketching a map on the walls. The walls became a moving, changing, panorama of people, events and places.

His concept of time became confusing. For in the time it took to sound one note of the music, a dozen different events took place on the walls. While the electric lightbulb pulsated through one of its alien heartbeats, whole tunes began and were ended on the record player. And while this was going on, the blood in Mac's body and the grain in the wood floor flowed incessantly through their endless rivers and streams.

— How are you feeling? Anna's voice drifted into his hearing. He thought the question over.

— Strange, great, human, not human, part of it all, not part of it. He said the words as each came into his mind and then wondered if he had really said anything. By this time he had forgotten the question.

— The world is on your walls. This time he made a conscious effort of speaking and listening to his voice. Anna laughed and poured more wine.

— I'll get some crayons, she said.

He watched her walk across the room, throwing her bad leg out before her. It made her seem to strut. He remembered the shocking things she had said to him in the bar. They didn't seem to have any importance now. His homosexuality wasn't real. It didn't matter. It was just another laughable game he had played. Anna came back with the crayons. They proceeded to draw a rough map of the world on the walls. Anna drew a blue America, Mac a yellow Ireland. Anna worked her way west from America while Mac worked east from Ireland. People began to arrive.

A young man wearing a long black overcoat was the first to arrive. He was stumbling drunk, protecting a bottle of whiskey. His lank hair was parted in

49

the middle and fell down over his ears. Sometimes
the hair swung across his face like curtains, framing
his nose. His overcoat came down to his ankles. He
stood in the middle of the room, arms crossed in front,
clasping himself, like a black monk. He considered
what was going on in the room then came over to
Mac and began telling him excitedly how to draw
Spain. He stopped talking to take out his bottle.
He resumed talking with his hands moving up and
down the form of his bottle. After feeling it for
a few minutes he carefully opened it. By now both
of them were staring at the bottle. Before going to
the kitchen for the glasses they both had a long drink.

— By the way, my name is Diarmuid, the young
man said when he came back with the glasses.

— I'm Mac.

— Wait till I tell you about Spain, said Diarmuid.
He picked up a crayon and drew in the provinces,
keeping up a running commentary about local customs here and there.

The door burst open and a wild young drunk
almost fell into the room. He had his arms wrapped
tightly around a brown paper parcel.

— Anna, he said.

His voice was hoarse with emotion. He threw
his parcel on the couch and went over to her.

— Anna, you're the salt of the earth. I had to
come out and see you. They're driving me crazy.
Jesus Christ, where's the drink? He let go her hands
and opened his parcel.

— Have you got a bottle-opener? he shouted.
Anna went to the kitchen to get one.

— Jesus Christ, he said as he poured out the

beer, I'm dying for for a drink.

They heard footsteps in the hallway and a whining male voice saying:

— I'm only trying to tell you how beautiful and intelligent I think you are.

— Fuck off and stop bothering me, an angry woman's voice answered. A second later she came through the open door.

— Henrietta, my darling, said Diarmuid. He gave her a hug. She took the glass of whiskey and slammed the door behind her.

— At least have the decency to come and talk this thing out with me, the male voice said through the door.

— Oh go to hell, please, said slim Henrietta. She took up a crayon and began writing on the wall.

People kept on arriving until both rooms were full. Some were so drunk they had to be supported on either side by their friends. Everybody brought something to drink. Scribblers were busy wherever they could find a clean piece of wall. The others stood around in tight, smoky groups talking in loud voices. The man who had been talking to God earlier on in the pub came into the room leaning heavily on a friend's shoulder. He was placed gently on the couch with a drink and a cigarette and went back into a trance immediately.

The sight of him made Mac think of Mona and then all that had happened during the day. Mac unwillingly let his mind bring him back to this morning. The cold, clear, black and white pictures followed one another, scene for scene. The decision he had made this morning flashed to his mind, as forceful and clear as ever.For the first time that day it frightened him. In the centre of this noisy, warm, roomful of people, he was getting sentimental . It's the drink, he thought. It's getting to me. I'm letting it take control. He forced the decision back to the forefront of his unwilling mind. He seemed to grow in size and, opening his mind to a sense of reason, he looked down over the rooms and the people in them.

Dear drunk, dirty people, he thought, I'm soon leaving your company, but I see that you're even more muddled and lost than I, and that I find unbearable. Have any of you got a map? Which of you has your seas charted? What port will you finally come to? Do you know how to navigate and find that port? Would you know what port it was even if you found it?

Mac, who had been a sailor, knew that all sailors are looking for something. That's the reason they spend long, boring, months cooped up in steel shells, ignoring things like money, family, government and earthquakes. Getting pissed up on week-long binges to convince themselves that they are totally free of all civilization's restraints. They never got even the tiniest bit free; merely disintegrated and in most cases, became bores; but they go on searching – either out of boredom or an imagined gift for notoriety. These people in the rooms, he found to be much like sailors. They were incapable of being captain; they would go along for the trip but never knew what course to follow.

When at fifteen Mac walked ashore in Sicily he had the sensation of having made a great voyage. I've made it, he said to himself, walking to the nearest bar and getting drunk. All Mac had done was scrub decks. The captain made it, but Mac could not lose the feeling that he had made an effort and accomplished something himself. In the bar, near the tanker berths, somewhere outside of Syracuse, the locals were suspicious and coldly polite. They played cards and watched every move in the bar. They were contemptuous of the amount that the sailors could spend in such a short time. For the locals this was just another slow weeknight, with three or maybe four cheap glasses of wine. Some were not even drinking. To the sailors this obscure little bar meant the half-way pissup stop between the Persian Gulf and Rotterdam — the home port. The voyage took three months and you couldn't get a drink in the Persian Gulf. Bandamashure was a place where a pipeline came out of the desert. There was nothing else there. They used to call it Banish-the-Whore.

Tanker berths were always miles from anywhere. A taxi to the nearest town and back would have cost Mac a week's wages. Except for that evening in Sicily he didn't get ashore until they were back in Rotterdam. There was a special bus that took him to a dance in the seamen's missions where the girls were outnumbered twenty to one. After three months scrubbing pots and decks he came home for Christmas with twelve pounds in his pocket.

Going to sea was not what he'd expected it would be. Those evenings spent by the fire, reading sea yarns instead of doing homework, he had envisioned himself snapping orders at menials and saving ships from certain destruction. He knew now that he would never even be an able-seaman because a doctor had discovered him to be colour-blind. Where did one find adventure as a member of the catering staff? He had come up against real snobbery for the first time and had been put very smartly in his place. The distance between officers and crew was unbelievable to Mac on his first trip.

The captain was another let-down; a fat idiot, dressed in white shorts and shirt, who crawled around the pantry floor on Sunday morning inspections looking for dust. The captain once told Mac that he was the most apt pantry boy he had ever met. Mac took it as a compliment but wasn't quite sure what he had meant. Everyone of the crew agreed that it had been an unusually bad trip, so Mac wasn't too disheartened.

Even if it was boring work on a ship, it was better than a messenger boy's job on a bike, which was what the other kids in the street were doing. And there was a strong possibility of getting some sex sooner or later. Mac went back to sea. He didn't like or trust the men he sailed with. He had a feeling they laughed at him behind his back. He thought this had something to do with the way he talked. He sometimes found himself using words that they never used. He felt himself to be different to others, but couldn't explain what the difference was. He learned to keep his thoughts silent after one or two outbursts of feeling, which embarrassed the company and brought down mockery on himself.

When he couldn't stand the sight of a crew any longer he left a ship. When he couldn't stand to be at home any longer he signed on another ship. So it went on for seven years, seven years of searching. He didn't know for what; if he had ever known then, he had long ago forgotten.

And still searching, Mac thought, looking round the room again. The dear dirty people were getting drunker still. All searching for something in the bottom of their bottles. Mac felt superior to everybody in the rooms. He felt vastly superior at that moment, more superior than at any other time. He remembered the beauty he had once seen in people's faces and felt sad. He knew that once he had been aware of the amazing capacity people had for beauty. And this awareness had made his thoughts beautiful. The honest eagerness on the face of a smiling deckboy as he whispered — 'Don't forget to lock the door.' And afterwards, his loyalty, when he treats you with casual nonchalance in front of the others on the mess-deck. He would never give the others any sign to indicate that anything is going on, nothing to indicate that at night you lie in each others arms and kiss. That kind of beauty he could not see on one face in these crowded rooms. The faces in the room were all marked, lined, too fat, or disfigured. They were used faces; the eyes burned; they were people on trips. They were just that little bit too hyper. They had suffered. All too plainly they had suffered, and some had even known destruction. There could be no beauty in this atmosphere. Beauty, when it was there, stood alone. It needed no extras to define itself. It just was. Unconscious and uncomplaining it stood around, waiting to be put to use. It wants to be used. Beauty wants to be put to work, to be part of the whole, compelling, natural function. These people in the rooms tried too hard. Their skin-tight faces were aggressive, their brotherly kisses were dangerous. Their intelligence was too razor-sharp. Their cut and thrust at each other could be mistaken for the real thing by a stranger, but they were indifferent and a little bored behind the cut and thrust. They were just keeping the endless game going, party games to pass the time.

Mac's brain began to function coldly. I still need barbiturates. He began to scheme after a quick check on the other possibilities. Gas. Head in the oven on a cushion. Plenty of shillings and the windows closed. No, that was too risky. Drowning. Swim out to sea. Keep going until you fall asleep and sink. The sea at night is cold, dark and lonely. No, no, not that; then . . . slit my wrists in the bath. But whose bath? There isn't one in the house. Somebody else's bath, and have them find a corpse in the morning? Freak the living daylight out of them. No, not the razor. I haven't the guts for the highjump, or the rope. I haven't a gun, or any hope of getting my hands on one. It must be the pills. Phone Mona now, a voice was telling him. Phone and make sure. She probably needs some persuasion. I hope to God she doesn't let me down, he thought, going into a sudden panic. Oh Christ, this is hell. Anything is better than this. But it has to be the pills, and going into a long, silent, peaceful blank sleep.

The question of cowardice never entered his head. Killing himself was the obvious, next and logical thing to do. Now his mind was made up. There would be no turning back. This he understood with finality. It was going to work, he should stay cool and try not to panic and it would be all right. It was so simple a course of action that it couldn't go wrong; get the pills from a friend and get out. What if she suffers afterwards? But isn't Mona going to suffer anyway? Isn't everyone going to suffer anyway? What possible difference could it make as to how you went? In a car or shot as an innocent bystander, or blown up in the war. The fall-out and old age and suicide are different ways of saying the same thing. Death is the word they say and only death. No death is ever glorious. Mac thought with clear vision; death is decay. A transformation after which we are unrecognizable dirt again. Recycling once more in the universe.

He went to the telephone in the hall. He dialled Mona's number. There was no answer. He was about to hang up when he realized he could phone any-body he wanted to. Was there anyone else he wanted to talk to? He stood for some minutes going over his list of people. The telephone was still ringing in Mona's flat. Brrr, Brrr — impersonally. He pictured himself as a ghost walking round Mona's flat and hearing the ringing there.

There was no one he wanted to speak to. He put the black mouthpiece back in its crutch. It looked to Mac like a question mark lying in its coffin.

He watched the scenes develop in the two rooms during the remainder of the night. He stood as a far-away spectator watching the pageant's unfolding. The people were going into a wild abandoned drunk. They knew they were in the presence of a large, free supply. The steady traffic went up and down the stairs, coming from and going to the toilet. A few were sick. Standing at the bottom of the stairs, calling Mona again, Mac would hear them retching. A young

57

man, dressed like a woman, fell through the glass pane
set in the upper half of the bathroom door. Blood
flowed down from a cut in his head and ruined his
makeup. He stood there on the stairs in a blood-
spattered mini-skirt crying. Will they have to cut my
hair off? he asked as he was being led out ot a car.

A small boy walked into the room screaming
with the full force of his lungs. It was Anna's son. She
took him back up to his bedroom. Mac went out to
telephone again. In the hall he heard the boy still
screaming upstairs and Anna's voice saying — now
I've fucked up two lives.

A fight had started and was stopped. Then
slowly, people began to drift out. Taxis were called
and lifts arranged and the sleepers were woken up.
Another day's drinking and working and talking came
to an end. They were going to their beds. Soon Mac
and Anna were standing in the empty rooms looking
at each other. Diarmuid was asleep on the floor
wrapped up in his long black overcoat.

— Is the child O.K.? Mac asked.

— Yes, he's O.K. now. He has nightmares.

Lying in bed, not touching, they stared at the
ceiling. Being in bed with a woman, Mac thought,
usually means having sex. Lying there, conscious of
Anna's breathing, he felt no desire for her.

— I'd like you to stay, Anna said.

— Yes, but . . Mac didn't know what to say. He
didn't want to tell her. He thought that Anna would
make a fuss and convince him to wait a while. And
then he would have to go through another day like
today all over again.

— I'd like to, he said, but I don't really know

where I am these days. I'll think about it when I straighten out.

His words seemed to hang over his head in the thick dark of the bedroom. He could nearly see the sentence. When he heard their echoes he knew they were the wrong words. They were so wrong that they would never be forgotten. He wished he could now say something that was right but he couldn't think of anything.

The bedroom door was opened and the little boy came into the room. He stood at the head of the bed in pyjamas.

— Mommy, he said, I don't like this place. He said it calmly, as if he had lain in the dark and thought it out.

— I know Peter, Anna said, we'll go away soon.

— Where?

— Australia. We'll go to your daddy in Austalia.

— Is he coming? Peter pointed a finger at Mac.

— No, just us. Now go back to bed.

— I'm afraid. Anna got up and took him back to his room. She didn't come back. Alone in the big bed, Mac slowly surrendered to sleep as the first hint of dawn began to outline the sparse furniture in the room.

CHAPTER 8

Mac woke up. A raw, grey light filled the room. As he became aware of Anna in the room he heard a seagull screaming. Dressed in her panties, Anna stood by the door biting her bottom lip in anger.

— What's happened? Mac asked.

— I found Diarmuid drinking a bottle of my whiskey. I broke it over his head. I'm getting to sleep.

She didn't allow her hysteria to show until she said sleep. She said sleep with the desperation of someone who hasn't had any for some time. She climbed into bed and got under the covers.

— I'd better go down and see how he is, Mac said.

He felt naked and exposed on the strange stairs in his underpants. He saw the thick blood on the broken glass of the bathroom door. The blood looked sordid and unreal in the now strengthening daylight. Maybe it won't be a corpse, he thought, going down the cold stairs; maybe she only knocked him out. He fully expected to find Diarmuid with his skull smashed.

Diarmuid stood in the front room looking at the floor. With a dazed expression on his face, he looked as if he might be listening to birds and angels singing. Bits of broken glass were stuck in his hair. Little streams of whiskey were drying on his face and dripping down the front of his overcoat.

— Hello, he said when Mac went over to him.

— Have you got a comb? Mac asked.

— Here you are.

Diarmuid took one from his inside pocket and gave it to Mac. He seemed cheerful.

— Are you hurt, asked Mac, combing the glass out of his hair, can you feel anything?

— No, I'm fine. Mac combed for a few minutes until he could see no more glass. He didn't find any cuts.

— You're lucky, he said, not even a cut.

Diarmuid took a beer bottle from an inside pocket.

— Have a drink Mac?

— Mac took a drink. It was whiskey. He felt a welcome, but slightly sickening glow start. After a night like that, he thought, the only thing to do is to drink away the horrible morning. He took another drink. Now he wanted to get away from Anna. Her breaking the whiskey bottle over Diarmuid's head was frightening. It was going too far. She could have killed him. That he might have found a dead Diarmuid here this morning made him shiver. Then reason returned to Mac's brain. Death, no matter how it happened, no matter who it happened to, was simply death. No one death has more significance than another.

He went back up to the bedroom and got dressed. Anna lay in bed. He hoped she was asleep. He wanted to be away.

— How is he? she asked.

— He's O.K. I'm taking him into town.

— Why?

— I'll see you in a few days. He lied, not wanting to explain why he was leaving.

She sat up and watched him walk to the door. She knows I'm frightened, Mac thought, his hand on the door knob, but I've got to get away. Keep going.

— I'll see you in a few days, he said again and ran down the stairs.

— We'd better go, he said to Diarmuid. Diarmuid had washed his face and looked drunkenly alert. They left the house quickly. Mac pulled the hall door shut and followed Diarmuid down the garden.

At the corner of the long, deserted road they waited at a bus stop and had another drink. In silence they watched for the familiar green doubledecker bus to take them warmly speeding to the city, out of this desolate suburb.

Standing with Diarmuid in the cold, raw morning, Mac thought about his first day at school. The weather that morning when he was four years old had been similar to this one. In his memory of that day long ago there was a grey windy morning with him being led through the strange streets by his mother's hand. Then his mother was talking to a tall figure in black. The figure in black reached down to take hold of him. He ran behind his mother. His mother grabbed him and pushed him towards the stranger. Mac broke free, and, terrified, ran off down the lane which seemed endless. The stranger chased and caught him. He was dragged across the lane and through a doorway in the high stone wall. When remembering this little scene of three figures in a lane long ago Mac could stand back from it and watch as if he were watching an old silent movie. Sometimes he would paint in colours and admire it as a picture. It was a blackgrey, bleak picture on the canvas of his mind. Why, he wondered, had the memory of his first day at school been imprinted so clearly? It was one of those memories he could never forget and to prove it, here he was remembering it on his last day.

He had hated everything about the convent. He hated walking to it on cold grey mornings with the taste of porridge in his mouth and a hot penny in his tight fist for the Black Babies. The punishment that warmed up his hands in chilly classrooms. And standing in line in the basement for lunch. The smell of burnt milk and the large boxes of greasy sandwiches.

— Won't be a minute, Diarmuid said, walking over to some bushes. He got back to the stop as the bus came into view.

They got off the bus at Stephen's Green and went into the Green to finish the whiskey. The sun came out and warmed them as they sat on a bench, looking at the pond. All kinds of birds and ducks went noisily about their morning's business. The fragrant smoke of burning leaves drifting past the bench made the whiskey taste better. Across the pond two figures approached another and the three stayed together making a group.

— The Legion of Mary, Mac said remembering yesterday, are out early.

— Oh is that who they are? Tell us, did you ever talk to them? Diarmuid was smiling now, perfectly at home in the new day.

— Yes, they cornered me yesterday. Mac took out cigarettes and lit up.

— They annoy me, Mac said, with their suspicions of evil and sin lurking behind everything and their long list of don'ts to help get through the wicked world untainted.

— I'm totally at the mercy of the big, beautiful, wicked world. Let it do what it likes to me, Diarmuid said and stood up.

— It must be near opening time.

Mac wanted to phone Mona. They started walking towards a gate. Insistent church bells tolled out the halfhour, barely making themselves heard above the traffic noise. Passing the public toilet Mac told Diarmuid a story about it. Diarmuid loved the story and began telling Mac one of his.

By the time they reached the pub they had related to each other the details of half a dozen sexual encounters with boys. Their tastes were so similar. Mac felt that Diarmuid was one of those people, like Anna, who had always been there, thinking similar thoughts, until one day you turned a corner and inevitably met them, and your existence before meeting appeared now to have been lacking in something. On an occasion like this Mac liked nothing better than to sit in a pub and drink with that person.

The pub was cool and quiet. They sat on stools

at the bar between two mirrored partitions. One other customer was sitting near the door in silence. A gas heater, painted silver with a lonely blue flame in its base, made the place look colder than it was. The stout barman walked noiselessly to stand before them. Sunlight coming through the large front window glinted on his spectacles making him eyeless. Behind him in the rows of shelved bottles, the liquids were a uniform amber, reflecting the rich dark woodwork.

– Two pints.

The barman nodded his head and went away. Mac and Diarmuid were talking about passionate boys in low voices when he came back five minutes later with the drinks. Mac paid, his heart glad that he had so much money today. They sat looking at the pints until the stout was black and settled with an even white collar on top. Then carefully they lifted the glasses, closed their eyes and drank.

– Ahh, that's better, said Diarmuid, putting the glass down. He put it down precisely on the wet ring where it had stood before.

– The first pint, said Mac lauging, it's such a holy ritual, like Mass.

– Exactly. Diarmuid raised his eyes to the smoke-blackened ceiling. I offer up this pint Lord, he prayed, and may there be a million more gorgious mornings to follow. Amen. Now let's get back to the sexual habits of middle class adolescents.

– Here's to the middle classes, Mac made a toast, for their well-behaved, clean, horny sons.

– I'll drink to that, said Diarmuid, where would we be without them?

Mac ordered two more pints.

— Did you ever get to hating your parents? God, mine are so stupid I can't believe they're real. They're nearly impossible to live with.

— Where else can you live if you don't want to work?

— Exactly. You've hit the nail on the what's it. Are you in the same predicament?

— Yes, answered Mac, for the moment, yes.

— Are you signing on the Labour Exchange?

— Yes. I'm getting unemployment. That's right! I've just remembered, today is payday. Mac let himself get excited about the fiver from the government. Then he remembered that he wouldn't be around to spend it. He had enough money for today in his pocket, so was it worthwhile going over to Gardiner Street? On the other hand why let the government keep its fiver? He felt compelled to go from habit. For the past two years on each Wednesday and Friday he had signed his name and collected the money. He decided to go today.

— The bastards won't give it to me; Diarmuid said, his voice bitter, when you really need it you can't get it.

Diarmuid sat staring into his pint. The barman stood at the window, his little finger moving slowly inside his nose. A cat with tiger stripes walked over to the heater and lay beside the warm metal. Mac could hear cars moving along the street. Inside all were silent. The large clock over the shelves of bottles gave the time as eleven.

Mac gave thought to the time and place he was in. Eleven on a Friday morning in July, 1969. I'm sitting at a bar in a city built on the mouth of a river, halfway down the coast of a small island, in the Atlantic ocean. There is no place in the world I want to go and nothing I want to do. I'm not hungry, as millions are. I've got average intelligence and looks and nothing to fear, except a long, boring continuation of my existence as it is now. That is what I find unbearable.

Going out every day, meeting the same people; they're all the same when you think about it, even Diarmuid here who's just a replica of myself, saying the same things, eating and shitting and making sure to be in the right place when someone buys a round of drinks. Going home at night, angry if the pubs are still open and you have no money; turning the key in the halldoor to see the family you don't talk to all staring at the television. You lie in bed not drunk enough to sleep, cursing through half the night at the unrelenting boredom of an existence that has no meaning — a senseless absurd void of repetition you move about in, making empty gestures.

The gestures you make towards the people you come into contact with. I like you. I hate you. I think you're intelligent. I think you're a fascist. Come to bed with me. Agree with me. And above all respect me. And when all is said and done, everyone finds himself alone, preoccupied with a secret image of himself that can never be expressed in words to another.

— Have another pint, Mac said.

Diarmuid lifted his head. The mirroring dark eyes were directed towards Mac's face but were seeing something far beyond. Something that was far into the future or distant in the past. He nodded his head as if struck dumb by what he was seeing. He's seeing his dismal future, full of nothing, and he's afraid. I'd better get out of here quick. Fear is contagious. Mac called to the barman for a pint. Diarmuid realised that Mac was about to leave.

—Don't go, he said.

— I've got to go, Mac said, the exchange closes at twelve. What's the matter? Does your head hurt?

Mac knew damn well what the matter was. The expression in Diarmuid's eyes reminded him of cattle in a slaughterhouse. The cattle waiting their turn knew what was about to happen, but fear prevented them from doing anything about it. They went along with the rest of the herd no matter what. Occasionally a beast jumps over the pen and fights the butchers. Mac regarded himself as the beast who was going to jump.

— Don't go, Diarmuid repeated, imploring now, his hands gripping Mac's coatsleeve. Mac was getting angry. He turned to pay the waiting barman.

— Is it the parting of the lovers? asked the barman.

Mac wanted to say things to Diarmuid, but not before this possibly-sneering barman. Dealing with Diarmuid, who still clutched his sleeve, and counting money for the barman threw Mac into confusion. He felt drops of sweat rolling down his arms inside his clothes. He pulled the hands away from his arm and walked out.

Mac hurried along Baggot Street, oblivious to traffic and people. He was saying aloud what he wanted to say to Diarmuid; don't cling to me, dear Diarmuid. Don't cling to ME. Sooner or later you're going to have to face it alone and I can't help you.

He took grim satisfaction from the force with which he uttered these words.

He collided with an elderly woman. Instinctively he put out his arms to steady her and himself. Partly in his embrace, she looked up to the terrible face. She let out a tiny yelp, clutching her bag to her chest. She was about to panic. Mac got away from her by crossing the street. On the other side he slowed down. He felt dirty and sweaty. He resisted the urge to disappear into the next cool pub; it was too close to Diarmuid.

He walked on, tired now as his anger cooled. sky was overcast again, the clouds a smooth blanket grey. A breeze ran along the pavement close to the ground; picking up a sheet of newspaper, it pasted the headlines across the fender of a parked car. 'SIX CATHOLICS KILLED IN BOMB BLAST' SECTARIAN MURDERS CONTINUE.'

Mac passed on. Grey day in Dublin; black day in Belfast. After so many such headlines as this, day in and day out, he no longer took any notice. He would go and collect his fiver, take a bath in Tara Street, smoke some hash and be sober meeting Mona.

CHAPTER 9

Mona woke early that Friday morning. She felt she had slept well, yet she had a vague memory of having travelled great distances in her sleep. The feeling of heavy oppression and dread with which she had gone to bed the night before was no longer there. Her head was clear.

She left the bed and dressed. Almost without thinking, she found herself half an hour later sitting at the typewriter, writing. She went clacking away at a great pace. The story which she had been trying to force along for the past six months now poured out of her. It seemed as if in one sudden leap she had jumped all the obstruction. She now knew she could do it. She would finish the book. That knowledge gave her mind energy and clarity.

Four hours later she left the typewriter, exhilarated and thirsty. She opened wide the one large window in the room. Standing at the window, taking breath after grateful breath of heady air, she saw the stunted, queer, dwarf of a tree in the garden. The garden was half the size of her room. The tree a gloomy prisoner in the wall's shadow.

She knew that the two knots on its skinny trunk were the eyes, she had watched them often before. Sad were the eyes, with wrinkles about them, and closed as if in pain. Looking at the tree she felt a growing sense of dissatisfaction within her. It was general at first and coming so soon after the exhilaration of writing, it puzzled her. Then slowly the feeling began to explain itself. It was dissatisfaction she felt with the high, dreary room which smelled of dampness, dissatisfaction with the stunted tree in the tiny, lifeless garden, with the bad weather of the last two weeks, with the sly looking landlady who went to mass every morning and smiled knowingly when she met Mona on the stairs. I know what's going on, the landlady's eyes seemed to be saying, I know you take men home to your bed. Nothing was ever said, of course, but sometimes the looks and smiles made Mona feel as if she was the biggest whore in the city. She had often found herself cursing the landlady's superior brand of piety.

I could get another flat, she thought, going to the partitioned corner of the room which served as the kitchen. She made a cup of instant coffee and discovered that she had no milk. Standing before the mirror over the mantle, fixing her hair, she realized it wasn't only the flat, it was the city. It was Ireland and it was Europe. She had been here too long, the charm was wearing off. She put her coat on and went out to get milk.

The fat woman in the store talked about the weather and overcharged her sixpence on the packet of biscuits. Mona stopped in the street outside. She looked at the pyramid-shaped milk carton in her hand. It was as if she was seeing that shape for the first time. It looked strange to her. The street looked strange; the people dressed in sombre clothes; the funny little motor cars; the fat woman's accent; all appeared strange. She felt alien.

— What the hell am I doing here? she asked herself, wanting to laugh. What am I doing here? This is ridiculous. I don't belong here. A year is enough. I should be moving on.

The sun came out for a few seconds then disappeared. She remembered her first sight of the city from the air and felt the thrill again of riding in the powerful jetplane. She wanted to be off. She longed to see the faces of home. Back in the room she sat down, the coffee forgotten. Excitement quickened her heart. She went out to the landing to piss. The flushing toilet was sudden and noisy in the silent house. She walked around the room several times quickly. She kicked the bed. In the dull light that was coming through the window the sheets were grey, the pillow twisted and flattened against the headboard. At the moment Dublin to her was cold, mean and dirty. She switched on the light and pulled her suitcase from under the bed. Her mind was made up. She was leaving.

— Give me one reason for staying here, she said aloud as she packed. Maurice can do what he likes about a divorce. It's worrying him, not me. I'm sick of being a mother to men-babies. Mac can have the pills. He doesn't want to stay with me, none of them do. I'm getting away from this bunch of neurotics.

straighten my own life out. The important thing now is to write, write and write. That's the only thing that matters. The world's full of people with petty problems, it always was and always will be.

She stopped packing to drink the milk. The travelling clock was beside the typewriter, showing the time two-thirty.

— Half two, she said, mimicking Mac's Dublin accent. I'd better get to the bank or I'll be going nowhere.

CHAPTER 10

She went to the bank in Grafton Street. It was
warm and sunny now, the day having finally decided
to be fine. She would get to the bank before it closed
at three; it wasn't far to walk. She would go to London
and stay with Margie Fletcher for a week. She got on
well with Margie, whom she had known since college.
Yes, it would be fun to see her again. To sit together
with a bottle of gin, talking far into the night, bringing
each other up to date about the happenings of the
past year. She would write to her parents from
London; the news would make them happy; then the
long flight up over the Atlantic, home to the good
old U.S. of A.

Feeling better with each step, she walked through
the mellow afternoon. She had that free, adventurous
feeling of a year ago, unattached, going somewhere and
writing.

Three big tourist buses pulled into the Shel-
bourne Hotel as she passed by. The tourists were
white- or blue-haired, wore plastic rain coats over out-

rageous clothes and looked at the scenery through either gold- or silver-rimmed spectacles.

— Had a good day ma'am? asked the green-uniformed, handsome doorman as he helped an old lady down from the bus. The old lady beamed.

— Wunnerful, thank you.

Behind her back the doorman winked at Mona. He thinks I'm a native, she thought, and sharing the joke.

— Hi, she said, letting him know she too was American and watching his face stiffen.

The quiet, elderly bankclerk handed over all the cash from her account.

— You're not leaving, he whispered, with shock and dismay registering on his face. It was as if he could not imagine anyone having reason to leave here.

— Afraid so, she said.

— Ah, that's too bad. Well, goodbye now and God bless.

He left her with the expression that he would lose sleep over her departure.

Back up narrow, bustling Grafton Street she went, delaying a while at her favourite bookstore window. Turning from the window she saw the graceful head of Justin McGarry moving towards her.

— Hello, he said, it's a lovely day.

— Yes, indeed it is. He seemed relaxed.

— Would you care for a drink?

— I'd love one, she answered, and meant it.

— You must forgive me for last night, he said as they got into step. You caught me off guard, I've always considered it bad taste to bore another with one's personal troubles. I must be getting old.

— No, no, it's me who should be forgiven. What right had I to call you and give you my troubles?

— I was pleased you did call. I can't remember the last person I talked to before yesterday. Let's forget the forigivings and get that drink.

The pubs were opening again and the one they went into was empty. Justin brought the drinks from the bar to a table. Mona settled down comfortably in her seat. The cross-channel ferry sailed at ten; she was in no rush now, anticipating a long pleasurable evening. A lazy flush of good feeling spread over her body.

— You're looking pleased and happy, Justin said as he sat down.

— I wrote again this morning.

— Did you now? Well here's to the old trade. They touched glasses and drank.

— Do you write now? She put the question delicately. She had heard he didn't from those who painted a sad picture of him with their words; she couldn't resist asking him.

— No. He wasn't upset by question, he seemed eager to talk. I've nothing to write about. Once it seemed I would never stop, I had so much to say. But that was long ago, when myself and the century were young. We started off together, myself and the century. We were both brand new. I felt then that I could change things, teach. After centuries of stupidity and ignorance the people were getting to their feet. Ireland most of all, I thought. Ireland would show the world what could be achieved in the face of oppression and prejudice. Socialism meant something then, I believed it was going to work and out of this wretched, blood-soaked island we would produce the first Socialist-Christian state. I felt as some kind of superman, full of strength, reason and intelligence. But I knew nothing of politics, or of people for that matter.

— After taking part in a world war and a civil war, I relearned what I had always known as a boy in a small village; the individual has no responsiblity whatsoever towards society and no one to answer to but himself and his creator, if he believes he has one. So I wrote because I believed it was what I had to do, as I'd believed I had to fight wars to save the world, or free Ireland. Writing was the only thing I wanted to do. I'd not have been happy doing anything else. When I wrote I felt as an animal must feel, a whole and perfect soul, completely in tune with its universe. And one day I stopped writing; as an old cow stops giving milk, I dried up. The whole thing, as I look back on it, is ridiculously simple. I laugh now at the torment I put myself through for mankind and myself.

He stopped talking and took a long drink of whiskey. Mona had nothing to say. She felt he had answered already any question she could have asked. Something about the simple direct way he had of putting things reminded her of Mac. Mac, as she had first known him, would sit with her for hours on afternoons like this telling her about his life on ships and fishing boats. She remembered Mac's high-pitched giggle and the shy side-glances he gave her when describing a situation which struck him as funny. That was Mac without the frown and hunched, tense shoulders, wrestling with the dog one day on the grass in the green.

She didn't feel upset or angry with Mac for what he was about to do; last night had been agonising before the blessed relief of two sleeping pills. What did one do when some one you knew wanted out? What could one do? Could anyone give to another a reason to live? No. It was and must be as Justin had said. Each must fight his own battles, on his ground, on his own terms. If the soul survived such battles, it could acquire an illuminating peace; if the soul didn't come through, it would be scarred. She began to understand that behind Mac's tortured reasoning there was a sense of logic. In some queer way, embroiled as he was in manic depressive confusion, he knew what he was doing.

She was no longer troubled by the idea that she had contributed in some way to his decision. Mac had made it plain, early on in the relationship, he desired nothing but her company. Neither of them had made binding promises, and neither wanted any. She felt envy for his strength, for strength it was, whatever the desperation from which it was conceived. The strength of purpose. Mac's purpose was misdirected, but he wouldn't be Mac if he didn't have that purpose. His nature made him view floating with contempt, it was either sink or swim. He had told her once that fishermen in cold northern waters didn't bother learning how to swim. If the boat sank and they had little chance of being picked up in the water, it was better to drown right away instead of hanging on to die from painful exposure.

— This friend you spoke about last night, the one who . . . Does he matter a great deal to you?

Her first impulse was to say oh yes, a great deal, but she hesitated, then could not answer. She realized she'd never asked herself that question. She would have to think about it.

— I . . . she lifted her hand off the table then let it drop down, I've never thought about it, she said. I mean . . . in some particular way he matters a lot, but not in the way I felt for my husband. I never worried about Mac, his life just seemed to roll along somehow. I knew he wasn't working or doing much with himself; I thought he would always be there, like Dublin, and I'm going to London tonight, then home. Does any of that make sense to you?

— Yes. Would you have any objections to company as far as London?

— None whatsoever; have you decided just this moment?

— Yes, I need to move and keep moving and shake off some cobwebs. There's nothing to keep me here.

— Where will you go? Mona asked, glad at the moment for having a destination herself.

— I'll probably travel a large circle, it doesn't matter. Any moment is better than inertia. Why do you look so frightened?

— I feel lost and very small. It's to do with Mac, I . . . .

Don't allow emotion to take over. If you do, then it will always be confusion. Think. Isolate the evil from the rest and show it clearly for all to see. I'm becoming a teacher again, maybe a writer; who knows? Well, it's time to get packed and write a few letters; tell a few friends abroad to make up a bed, McGarry's going the rounds again. I'll see you on the boat. Is it the Liverpool Ferry you're taking?

— Yes, at ten.

— Don't lose your way in the meantime. Bye.

Mona watched him walk out the door. I'm going to miss these pubs she thought, really miss them. She finished her drink.

CHAPTER 11

Mac stood in the queue at hatch number five. There were hundreds of men in long lines before each of the twenty hatches. The ages of the men ranged from eighteen to sixty. They were dressed in old suits or threadbare overcoats, their looking-for-work uniforms. Mac could smell the men around him, the sweet smell of unwashed bodies. The lines moved slowly. A large genial-looking policeman surveyed the long high hall from his place beneath the clock. It was eleven-fifteen.

Mac looked slowly about at the coughing, foot-shuffling, mainly silent crowd. How many of them are my age, born in the same month, in the same hospital? Perhaps I lay as an infant beside that fellow over there, the one staring at his feet. A journey lasting a quarter of a century from hopeful birth to this. I've never spoken to anyone here. I know that none of them has anything interesting to say. All they could do is echo my own life, or even less. If there was a war on then I'd be in the trenches beside them. Always the same faces. You meet them in school, in the factories or here, and you'd probably meet them in a doss-house when they're seventy.

If you're signing on the Labour at twenty-five, there's a strong possibility you'll be signing for the rest of your life. That's true. They lose the habit of work. They sit around their mother's house thinking, or do they think? They must think. What's happened to my life? That must be the common denominator. Why did my life never get off the ground? Most of them here will spend the afternoon sitting in the movies. Then home to cheese sandwiches and tea. Stepping past someone sitting on the house-steps in the sun. Another week over, nothing gained, nothing lost, starting Monday do it all over again. What's happened to my life?

Mac stood at the hatch, presented the card, signed twice and took the slip to the cashier. Slim fingers flicked five times. He pushed the crisp new notes into his pocket as he walked out.

He turned to the right in Gardiner Street, going towards the Customs House. Now that he was near the house his thoughts turned to his family. It would be all over by the time they got back. Nothing like what was going to happen had touched their lives before. There had been deaths of course, the grand-mother's, but that had been old age. They had taken it well, had even been relieved. But this, suicide — it was something he was sure they had never given any thought to. It didn't enter their world; they were practising Catholics. It must appear to them as the greatest sin there is.

He turned again and approached the house.

The house looked eerie under the overcast sky. Like a skull with the three windows as two empty eye-sockets and an open mouth. Then of course there were the neighbours, of whom his mother was constantly aware. She hated for them to know anything about the family which she regarded as private. The circumstances of his death were going to cause her endless mortification. It wasn't much of a return after a life-long struggle raising him. However, he could not allow their feelings to stand in his way. That would be stupid. They believed in a god who cared for and looked after them. That belief would carry them through.

He turned the key in the lock and went in. On the floor in the hallway lay a postcard. He picked it up. In his mother's handwriting on the back was written — 'Having a wonderful time. See you soon.' He turned the card over. The picture had green mountains, blue sea and white houses. This was their first holiday since he had been a child. They would come back to find a corpse. That's their problem, I'd better stop thinking about them before I lose the courage.

His body began to shake from the knees up. He sat down in the armchair. At first he tried to control his body. With clenched fists he pressed his feet to the floor saying, Stop it, Stop it, Stop it. Then he relaxed, lay back and shook. After a while it stopped. He took the remaining lump of hash from his top pocket. It'll blast you out of your skull, the dealer had said. He rolled a big one, his hands steady now, mixing in tobacco with the Lebanese Gold. This will get me above it all, he said, and lit up. He inhaled and held in the warm cloud of smoke deep in his lungs as if he were doing breathing exercises. He felt the potent cloud being absorbed by the lungwalls, tasting the Lebanese sun which had given life to the plant. In a short while it would take effect on his mind.

His body demanded food. He refused. There would be no food today for this body. You have had enough, the brain said to the stomach. You will never eat again. He felt thirsty and stood up, light-headed, to make tea. The steady drone of the factory continued outside the kitchen window. My father's place of work, he said aloud, I refused to do it. After six months in the chocolate factory I stood here in this kitchen, father was eating his dinner at the time, and I refused to work. He could still remember the look on his father's face that day. This wasn't the first time he had said that, it was the last time. After count-less jobs, Mac meant it. His father kept on spreading butter on a slice of bread. I don't know what you're going to do then, he had said, you have to work for money. They don't give it to you for nothing.

His father had never mentioned the subject again. His mother did, often. When are you going to go out and get work? she used to say in a severe voice. She usually said this while gutting fish or peeling potatoes in the morning. Do you want me stuck in a factory for the rest of my life doing something that I hate? Mac would answer her. Everyone else has to do it; it's time you woke up to that, and turn down that music, it's giving me a pain in the brain.

Mac drank his tea looking at the kitchen; the radio on the shelf with rubbish and old bills piled up behind it; the gas stove where food for seven people had been cooked every day for eighteen years; the kitchen table where they ate, a heap of shoes underneath; the wood along the wall he had painted cream the first year they moved here, and nearly every year since. It was easy to become sentimental. I'd better watch that, he reminded himself, this is no time to be doing it. The old house was due to be torn down soon and then it won't matter what I painted cream. There will be a heap of rubble and dust and the family will move away somewhere, leaving my ghost behind.

He had no trouble putting all thoughts of his family from his mind. He shut the door to that part of his memory completely. I'm alone, he told himself, there is no other way to do it. None of the human weaknesses can be allowed to interfere. My will must be as hard and unrelenting as steel. Concentrate on getting through this one act tonight and it's all over. After tonight I will have a peace that cannot be broken.

What a fool I have been he thought, smiling. Writing to the Voluntary Overseas Organizations. Send me anywhere, I said, I'm no longer interested in making money. I want to help the world. But you have nothing to offer, they had written back, you are an unskilled labourer, the same as the natives. I felt like the biggest fool in the universe. There's a hundred other things I could blush about. I'm not going to. I've paid enough for my blunders in their rotten, corrupt world. The incredible mess which is mankind is not worth another thought, he decided.

— I will take a bath, for I must be clean. Then once more I will walk, a drugged, smiling fool among the other fools, but this time I'll be laughing.

He took towel and soap and left the house. Noisy,

heavy afternoon traffic filled the centre of town. Big trucks hauling to and from the nearby docks belched fumes into his face. He stood a long time at street corners making sure it was safe to cross. Under Butt Bridge, small islands of filth rose bubbling to the surface. The stench of the low tide was strong in his nostrils. The tired, dirty river carrying its overload of refuse to the sea. Mac, the old sailor, had steamed downriver many times on those earlier voyages to escape from depressing, endless streets. The voyage always ended back in Dublin, no matter where he had gone. He knew it could never be otherwise for him. It was pointless trying to be an exile if you were not cut out for it. When living abroad, his soul ached one hundred times a day to be sitting by the Liffey drinking Guinness. Now that he was back he couldn't live in the reality of the place. He couldn't live with it — he couldn't live without it. That fatal charmer was going to devour one more soul.

In Tara Street Public Baths the noise was deafening. Lying in an old marked bath upstairs, it seemed to Mac as if all the people in the world were down in the swimming pools. Gradually the sounds became a dull roar. He was hardly conscious of it. It was the same sound he heard when holding a sea-shell to his ear as a child. Listen, his mother had said, you can hear the tide coming in. The child had listened for hours and wondered; what was that sound you could hear all the time, forever and ever?

Mac was dozing in the warm bath water. A whistle blew. The hour was up for the swimmers. After dressing in the shapeless clothes he left the bathroom. A large old man was seated on a chair outside on the balcony; gazing with dreamy eyes at the open-fronted cubicals down below where the kids dressed.

— Lookee, no touchee, Mac said to him. The man didn't seem to hear. His eyes never left the kids.

CHAPTER 12

Back in the house again, Mac hung the wet towel on the clothesline in the backyard. He went upstairs to get his suitcase; in it he kept his personal belongings. He carried it down to the front room and laid it open on the floor. He threw all the letters and photographs into the fireplace. These were followed by sheets of foolscap he had covered with writing one sleepless night when trying to get the frustrations he felt down on paper. He lit a cigarette before carefully burning the papers. He wanted everything of a personal nature destroyed, wishing the people who knew him to forget him as quickly as these papers burned. Anything left behind was sure to be misunderstood. He put the kettle on to make tea; Mac seemed to be always thirsty. He was moving about now slowly; his usual staccato, impatient way of handling objects was replaced by a lingering touch. He fondled a cup as he washed it, marvelling at his hands. Going to the teapot, he became aware of his feet. They seemed far away, moving independently across the floor, miles away from his eyes. He seemed to grow incredibly vast in stature. The floor was now the world; he stepped across continents to the table. A fly walked along the sides of the sugarbowl. The enormity of the living universe held him enthralled. He seemed to see the fly as if he were a fly. Suddenly, sharp sunlight filled the room.

— I'm alive, he said, alive.

For a few moments he felt he was close to understanding something. He didn't know what it was. He had an image of his brain as a jewel. Something was about to be made clear. His hand reached out and slowly came down to crush the fly on the table. He turned his hand to see, as the image of the jewel faded. Going to the sink he could now feel the tiny mess on his skin. He washed his hands, watching the crushed fly flow down the drain. In the mirror over the sink he saw his puzzled face, the hair tangled from the bath. When he'd finished combing his hair he'd forgotten the strange feeling of a minute before in the kitchen. He wanted a drink.

He picked his way through the people waiting for buses in Abbey Street, women with full shopping bags, children eating chocolate, Christian Brothers showing patience as they waited for the number twenty-two, a navvy in his workclothes, already drunk, trying to light a cigarette and hold on to his parcels at the same time. Chrome on the cars reflected the sun. Buildings reflected in the windows of buildings opposite. It was the Friday evening rush-hour.

I'll go into the first pub, he thought, wait till it's over. There's no comfort crossing the town in this crowd. He sat at the bar waiting for his drink. He had never used this pub much. It was too close to home. When he got drunk he didn't like to be near the house where the neighbours knew him. It was better to be across the river away from them all.

Behind the bar there was an enlarged photograph of an old theatre. Three women had been photographed in front of the theatre. Judging by their clothes, hair styles and shoes it must have been taken in the forties. Two of the women were coming towards the camera fullface. The third was walking past the theatre door towards the left side of the photograph. One night when drinking in this bar, a man who lived in the neighbourhood told Mac that the third woman in the picture committed suicide shortly after it was taken. She had lived a few doors down the street. Mac couldn't remember what the man had said her name was. Her profile was blurred because of the distance from the camera. She had dark brown hair and a grey coat reaching down below her knees. One leg was out in front; the heel just touching the ground and a small black bag was held under the arm.

Where was she going? Perhaps the cinema in Talbot Street. She was going in that direction, or going to a church; to ask for relief from the agony her soul felt. Or going to meet a friend to sit and talk. There she was now, twenty years later, hanging above the bar for all to see. That theatre had been across the street. It had burned down and been replaced by a much larger building. The new theatre was named after the old one. She hadn't walked very far.

The bar had been redecorated. They were all at it now. Pebble-dashed buff walls, low wooden ceiling with inset lights, carpets, the micro-wave sandwich cooker screamed to announce another cellophane-covered sandwich toasted. The barman hummed along with the movie themes coming from behind the curtains. The 'passing trade' sat stiff, staring at the bottle labels. A group of workers argued about the strike beginning Monday. Mac sat staring at the photograph.

The dreariness of the people around him filled him with disgust. He thought of the years he had spent with people like this in factories, hotels and ships, the nothings they forced themselves to become during the eight-hour shift, talking about the job for another four hours when they got together for a drink. If they weren't complaining about the job the conversation was about football and television. And the thousands of tourists who came and found the place charming until you were more disgusted with the gawking tourists than with the dreary workers. Smiling tourists having a good time examining the circumstances of your unendurable life.

Myself, in Barcelona, a tourist, walking around for a month, drunk on cheap brandy. Soberano, that was the name of the stuff. Looking at people's lives in the Barrio Chino, sharing a room on Calle Escudiliers with Juan, the little queen from Cadiz, all I could see there was misery. These people are animals said a German one night. Me alone, no Spanish, dumbly watching life. Going down to the docks to see if there was a ship I could get the hell out on. An elderly Australian telling a ship's captain that he wasn't too old for a deckboy's job at ten pounds sterling a month.

Drunk, standing in the street at two in the morning, clapping hands for the sereno to come and let you in with his key. Hardly talking to anyone for a month. Embrace Juan when he comes home from the bar. Oh, senor! Turn him over, lift up his nightie. No, no senor. Taking the train back to German Switzerland. Again a waiter fourteen hours a day in a clean precise Swiss hotel. Fined ten francs for being late ten minutes in the morning. The Sicilian dishwasher showing me his gun. Me no afraid. You my friend. Yes Antonio I'm you're friend. I lost control one day, stabbed a cook through the hand.

Back to London. No friends. Working in a hotel. Spending two days off every week in bed. Going up to Camden town once or twice to see sad Irishmen crying into their beer. Couldn't talk to them. These countrymen always dreaming of small farms, hating everything about their lives as I hated everything about mine. I didn't want to be identified with them. Stayed alone for six months. That Irish girl worked as a chashier. in the hotel; said why don't we sleep together. No, I said, don't want to get involved. Went home with the German waiter instead. That was a mistake, couldn't look him in the face next morning. Left before he woke up. Had to leave the job; people were getting too close. They knew too much about me. Everybody I met in London seemed to be lonely. The place became unbearable. Sitting in the room in Victoria, thinking of the people you worked with and how lonely they all were, longing for it to be different, yet when someone asked you to come home for a drink you always had an excuse ready. Couldn't deal with human contact. Then suddenly running for the boat-train to get out of London. Felt yourself going mad, wanting to strangle a customer in the hotel the day before.

How small and dirty Dublin always looked from the train. Mother, looking older and greyer, opened the door the morning you got back. You fell into the old bed again, with no more of a future now than you had two years ago when you left, the taste of the world you went off to find and couldn't deal with, bitter in your mouth. Nothing was any clearer, the brain a muddle of place names and faces you want to forget. You had home, and sanity, and sleep.

The pub clock made it seven. Time for one more here, then Mona. He motioned to the barman with his glass. How many drinks in ten years? He did some calculations on a beermat. Probably fifteen thousand. Why did I never get bored? Here I am taking stock at the quarter century mark. What must it be like at ninety? I'll be spared that. He finished the drink and walked out.

There was less traffic now. He moved through the warm evening. His feet treading easily the well remembered pavements. Turn right at the Liffey, past long queues for the cinemas. Men in suits were taking their dates to the pictures on this paynight. They were dressed to kill, waiting half an hour to get in. Over O'Connell Bridge Mac went, dodging the tinkers begging. The spires up in the Liberties stood out against the colourful sunset. Around the bridge were the neon lights, many coloured and the noise of loudspeakers at a political meeting.

Two men came down Westmoreland Street with long faces. They had the same features, must be brothers. One tall, one shorter. As far back as Mac could remember they had walked the city streets.

Maybe they did nothing else. Wearing caps and overcoats, with their hands behind their backs, always with the same measured tread, never talking they tramped on forever.

A madman directed the sparse traffic at College Green. Under the monstrous soot-blackened columns of the Bank of Ireland a pavement artist was busy on hands and knees.

He walked past Trinity's front gate, his thoughts now on Mona. He knew she would have the pills. He had a feeling she would. She had always kept her word in the past. There is no one else he knew as dependable as she was or as strong that way.

Mona was sitting in the lounge near the door, an empty glass before her.

— Hello.

— Hello Mac.

— Have a drink?

— No Mac, I can't stay, I have . . . what you asked me for.

She paused with her hand on the clasp of her bag.

— Well give them to me.

— Are you sure Mac?

— Positive.

He watched her take a white envelope from her bag and put it on the table.

— Goodbye Mac, she said and walked out.

Out on the street again, capsules in his pocket, he went towards O'D's on Merrion Row for a drink.

CHAPTER 13

On the floor in Anna's house tiny splinters of glass caught and held the fading daylight as it receded from the back room. Sitting on the couch under the window she could hear Peter, her son, talking to himself in the garden. The pinpoints of gleaming glass reminded her of the sun on the island of Hydra a year before. She didn't want to remember that. Hydra had been one of the places she had gone to, and came away from, looking for somewhere else.

Shadows gathered at the tops of the walls. The world drawn on the walls the night before, seemed to shimmer as if moving in the uncertain light. At first America seemed to stand out more clearly than the rest, than Europe, than the middle east. It seemed as if the road of her life had been illuminated in sequence. She sipped her whiskey.

She remembered herself at twenty-one, with that confidence one has at twenty-one, dressing in front of the mirror at home, her uncles downstairs making jokes. Her mother cried and told her a hundred times not to go to Germany. Standing in front of the mirror, she saw a tall goodlooking figure who couldn't stop that huge idiotic smile. The ticket to Paris was snug in the passport. She had endless amounts of money in her name. The expensive luggage lay around, filled with new clothes. She could go everywhere and anywhere she wanted to. The world was out there to be enjoyed.

Three months later in Paris she had married Jan. Looking back at it now it still seemed as if it could have worked out. She would have stayed with him, she still wanted him, even now. But to be honest with herself, as she could be now, she knew that an important part of her getting married had been to escape the horror of lonliness she had always felt. Her grand plan of travel through every country in Europe, or anywhere else, she could not accomplish alone.

Jan was a painter. A very frustrated painter who didn't believe he would ever be capable of getting down on canvas the brilliance and intensity of his visions. He didn't believe there was a painter living with an intensity such as his. After he was married he realized, but would never admit, that he lacked the patience and devotion necessary for developing his talent to its fullest. Yet he wanted to be granted an exhibition and have his paintings sold, as other painters did at their exhibitions. He considered the work that most of his contemporaries sold to be rubbish. The whims of a stupid public decided who was to be the most popular painter. The public, which wouldn't buy his stuff on a whim (he considered himself as good a craftsman as any), infuriated him.

They broke up because he wanted to be some-where else, without her. He went to Australia, which was as far away as he could get. She didn't waste time thinking about it. She knew now she should have gone home as they had begged her to. At home she wouldn't have had to make a decision. Alone in Europe she made a decision immediately. She took the pills. With only a wrecked marriage she might have gone home, after a time. But, with a wrecked marriage, a suicide attempt, a bum leg that no amount of money could fix and a baby on the way, going home was out of the question.

With that list of disasters, she never wanted to see her family again. Exiled a year after leaving home, she drifted about. She gave parties almost every night, wherever she happened to be living. Parties filled up the empty houses. She expected nothing more from men than sex, and this confused them. She wasn't just another rich woman picking up studs, she was a generous friend; but from the start they could see that she didn't believe this man-woman relationship was going to be anything more than friendly sex. Men who accepted this readily with other women, demanded more from Anna. They saw possibilities of a wife-mother-friend-family security and good-times arrangement, everything a man could want. She wasn't having any of that, and after failing to get her seriously interested, they soon left with hurt egos.

Peter came in from the garden. Groping about in the dim room, he found her on the couch. He was hungry and frightened of the falling dark. She switched on the lamp and drew the curtains. He munched away

on the packet of frankfurters she gave him. He refused
to let her cook them. If she had insisted on cooking
them he'd have had a screaming fit lasting for hours.
She hadn't the energy to oppose him anymore. Sometimes she felt he hated her. As if he knew that he had
been shortchanged somewhere, that she wasn't doing
her job.

His eyes, she felt, accused her all the time of
being a failure. It had gone too far to convince him
otherwise. He had taken control of his young life like
a tyrant. He demanded the things necessary for his
development. When she couldn't meet his demands
he punished her. He made her life unbearable by constantly running away. He would look at her from the
corners of his eyes while deliberately dropping plates
of food on the floor. He was strong for his age, and
often attacked her physically. In a few more years
she knew he would beat her up. Her life was as domi-
nated by this four year old as no man could have done,
and there was always the knowledge that she hadn't
wanted him, that she had even tried to kill him before
he was born, to haunt and torture her. Yet, he was
all she had and after he was gone she would be lonelier
than before.

She poured herself another drink. Peter turned
on the television. Soon, she decided he must be sent
to his father in Australia. She would have to let him
go, completely. It was better for them both not to
see each other for a long time. There was no other
way; she had delayed too long already. Peter would go
to begin all over again with a father he had never
known. That would be painful for a child; or would it?
At least his father wanted him. It would probably

work out for them. There was no chance of reconciliation between herself and Jan. Not even a hint of it in his letters.

Tomorrow, then, she would phone the airlines to see about sending him. A letter to Jan telling him when Peter was arriving and it was done. Put Peter on the plane and wave goodbye. What then? Where will I go? Her mind went blank. She poured a drink and watched television with her child.

CHAPTER 14

The taxi sped along deserted streets on its way to the ferry. Justin McGarry in the back of the taxi was indecisive. As he watched the bleak dockland roll past the window, he still didn't know whether he would take the boat or not. He had nearly managed to persuade himself that he was coming down to see Mona off. It was always during this taxi ride to the boat that the city he was leaving appeared warm and intimate and seemed to be pulling him back.

It took all his willpower not to shout stop, as they passed the cosy looking lights of a public house. I've got to go, he told himself, got to keep going and keep interested. Only thing to do. Anything can happen and it usually does, but I've got to make the effort.

— Pull over here, he said to the taximan. It was the last pub before the boat.

— Come in and have a drink.

Standing at the bar with a glass of whiskey, Justin was playing with the idea of having a few drinks and taking the taxi home to go to bed. A picture was in his mind of the cold, rolling nightsea, which lay ahead of him if he went. It was looking at the middleaged drinkers at the bar that made up his mind. They were so stagnant. Sitting there like bits of furniture; they obviously were never going anywhere again.

— Blast it to hell, he said to the driver, I'm sixty-five and I'd rather die running up a steep mountain. Take me to the boat.

It was after he had taken a cabin and was walking the deck, when he realized the effect his words had had on the taxi driver.

— He must have thought me raving mad, he said, and laughed.

He kept on laughing, remembering the driver's face. He hadn't laughed like this for years. There was no one else on that part of the deck except for Justin in convulsions, hitting the ship's rail with his open hand. Eventually he was able to stop. He wiped his eyes and listened to the suck and slap of the water between the ship and the wall.

Across the dock the regularly-spaced lamps threw pools of light on the still, black water. The air was clear and sharp. Justin buttoned up his overcoat. He felt already as if he were halfway between two places. The reclaimed land the dock was built on was too recent to invoke memories. It was a departure point which as yet was not properly named. He wasn't only leaving Dublin, Ireland; he was beginning a circle from a new, nameless place.

He heard a whistle blow twice. Then the thudding propellers pushed the ship from the wall. She lay motionless for a few moments in the centre of the dock. Again the propellers kicked, and she moved forward into the river. Smiling now, Justin went to look for Mona.

CHAPTER 15

Mac's brain was quiet now. He was sure everything was going to be all right. He didn't want to go home and take the pills in broad daylight; there was something unnatural about that. Better to wait till dark, until the day was over.

He pushed open the door and entered the noisy bar. It was packed, the bodies thrust against each other all the way down the narrow bar. A hundred flushed faces were reflected in the mirrors and many feet tapped to the wild, shrill traditional music from fiddles, flutes, mandolins and tin whistles. Five barmen were kept busy running and pulling pints.

This was where he had really started to drink eight years before, during the few months home between ships, and while the money lasted. Sitting here every night, listening to the music that had just been revived in Dublin, the thrill of discovering your national sound and soaking yourself in it for as long as you liked. Nothing else seemed to matter then, apart from the music and drink. He would go anywhere to hear it, staying up drinking until four in the morning, or all night.

The music didn't do for him now what it had then. It was still good, but he no longer felt the fire it used to kindle in his heart. That was gone, and gone too the quick thumping heartbeats he used to feel on the days he signed on a new ship. So many things were gone. He had peeled through layers of experiences until there was nothing left. He had found the person he believed to be his true self and didn't like that person. There was nothing in the world he could use now to cover up that self he had exposed.

The noisy crowd pushed him back and forward. Mac allowed himself to be pushed around as they squeezed past. The music went on, following itself around in circles. Each tune was played a certain length of time, then ended abruptly. After a short rest another one started. It was hard to tell how some tunes were different from others, they sounded so alike; but, only the experts cared. The people loved the sound, that was enough. Not resisting the flow of life about him, Mac soon found himself at the door. That's what happens, he thought, when you don't fight, you're pushed out the door. You're either in or out, and if you want in, you must fight and struggle with the rest. They have no time for you if you're not prepared to be involved. People who drop out are soon forgotten.

He leaned against the window outside in the street. It was getting dark. Strollers passed by in the dim light. When the pub door was opened to let someone in he heard the music for a few seconds; the street became quiet again as the door closed. Time to go home, he said, but he didn't move. Little man you've had a busy day; his mother used to say that when she put him to bed. It made him smile to remember. He straightened to go.

— Ya fuckin' did touch me up, I'll bleedin' kill you. The voice came from further down the street. Mac saw three figures struggling in a doorway.

— I didn't mean anything by it. What are you getting so angry about. Two of the figures were punching the third. The one who was being beated fell on the pavement where he was kicked several times. As Mac walked towards them the two on their feet ran off. The figure huddled in the doorway was wearing a long black overcoat. Mac knew who it was.

— Diarmuid, they're gone. Can you stand up?

— Wait a minute. Oh Christ. Mac lifted him to a sitting position.

— Take your time. Get your breath. Diarmuid sat shaking and gasping for breath. His nose was bleeding and inside his mouth was cut. Mac pressed his handkerchief to the bloody nose. The street light came on, showing Diarmuid's face to be ghostly white.

— Lean your head back, that's it. Mac pulled the head back by the hair. The whites of the eyes staring up at the sky.

— I think it's stopped now. Can you stand up?
Diarmuid stood up, leaning on Mac's arm.

— What did they want to do that for? We were getting on great. I don't understand these people. Do you?

— They have a thing about being touched. It gives them an excuse to beat people up and they know the law will be on their side if they're caught at it.

Haven't you figured that out yet? Surely you know by now? Mac was angry that Diarmuid had been kicked, and angry with Diarmuid for putting himself in a position to be kicked.

They were outside another pub. Mac pushed Diarmuid in before him.

— Go and wash the blood off, I'll get you a drink.

— What happened to him? the suspicious barman asked Mac.

— Someone hit him.

— He was in here earlier. Was it them two fellas he was with?

— I don't know, Mac answered. Give us two small whiskies.

— I don't want any trouble in here.

— There's no trouble, whoever it was that hit him has gone.

The barman poured the drinks. Mac paid and sat waiting for Diarmuid to come out. The damn fool. Why can't he look after himself. With his stupid philosophy of letting life do to him what it will, and his innocent approach to it all. Making passes at street-kids who liked nothing better than to kick his head in. Is he trying to be a saint or something? Going about trusting everybody, believing in their goodness. He's harmless himself and thinks everyone else is. Or maybe he knows better and does it anyway. Mac remembered some of the conversation he had had with Diarmuid the night before at Anna's house. He seemed to know what he was doing. He was intelligent. He had read a lot and retained what he read. As Mac thought about Diarmuid, he became convinced that Diarmuid knew exactly what he was doing. He wasn't a fool; he must have chosen to go through life as a drunken football.

Diarmuid came out of the jacks. His right eye was puffed and discoloured. There was dust on his coat from the street. He didn't seem too upset by what had happened. When he smiled Mac saw the jagged end of a broken tooth.

— Drink that. Mac handed him the whiskey.

— Thanks. He drank, making a face when the spirits stung the cut in his mouth.

— You've been through it today, Mac said.

— Oh, don't pay any attention to that, Diarmuid touched his swollen face.

Still looking into Diarmuid's face Mac seemed to see the quiet, old streets through which he would soon walk to the house. Inside the house would be cold: colder than the streets. And the stillness he would feel emanating from the walls and clustering up about the high ceilings. And the framed photographs on the walls in the front room. There was one of him as a baby with clenched fists and a tuft of fair hair over a big grin: the parents on either side like wooden statues with high, wavy hair.

And on the polished table, between the bowl of plastic fruit and the ashtray, he would place the red and black pills. How would he get them down? Difficult — so many, so big. Whiskey would be best to make sure. Whiskey it would be. Filling the tumbler, and one at a time gulp and swallow twenty, and up the stairs to bed. Where he would be warm and safe, and home.

— I've got to be going. He bought the whiskey

from the barman and put the five pound note in Diarmuid's hand.

    — Compliments of the government, Mac said. Good luck.

His Resumé

Those were the best years, but he was so remote
no one could touch him. And when those he knew
at the time tied him on the strand and gathered round
to inspect him with embarrassed curiosity he didn't
mind: looked at the sky, even forgave in advance as he
knew some would like to hurt – and they did. They
used physical pain which was kinder, but still they
never touched him which was what he wanted most.
That rope tightening about his chest as someone fell
back in senseless laughter at the enormity of the act
they were engaged in. The naked form of one they
dare not touch bared to the universe and God. The
organs prodded with sticks and jokes and lassoed with
bits of rope. And patiently he accepted the torment
which he knew long ago he would always receive, and
wished they had the courage to rape him decently now
he was tied helpless.